The Tramp Room

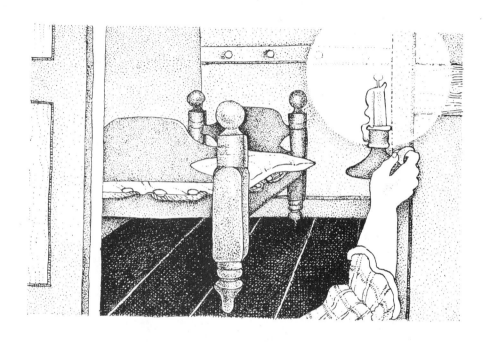

The Tramp Room

by Nancy-Lou Patterson

Joseph
Schneider
Haus

Friends of the Joseph Schneider Haus

Wilfrid Laurier University Press

Publication of this book was made possible in part by funding from the Friends of the Joseph Schneider Haus.

We acknowledge the support of the Canada Council for the Arts for our publishing program.

We acknowledge the financial support of the Government of Canada through the Book Publishing Industry Development Program for our publishing activities.

Canadian Cataloguing in Publication Data

Patterson, Nancy-Lou, 1929-
  The tramp room

ISBN 0-88920-329-6

I. Friends of Joseph Schneider Haus. II. Title.

PS8581.A79T72 1998   C813'.54   C98-932629-2
PR9199.3.P37T72 1998

Copyright © 1999 Nancy-Lou Patterson
WILFRID LAURIER UNIVERSITY PRESS
Waterloo, Ontario, Canada   N2L 3C5

Cover Photo: Joseph Schneider Haus Four-Square Kitchen Garden. Photo: Bill Knetsch, The Studio, Guelph. FIRST PRIZE, Friends of the Joseph Schneider Haus Photography Contest 1997

Text Illustrations: Nancy-Lou Patterson

Cover Design: Ampersand Studios

Printed in Canada

In memory of
my grandmother
Emma Wanger Gellerman
1878–1954

This story is a work of fiction. Every effort has been made to achieve accuracy of detail in regard to the nineteenth century community and culture it represents. The names of the Joseph Schneider family, whose home is now the Joseph Schneider Haus Museum, have been used, but their characters as I have portrayed them, and the experiences they are described as having, are entirely imaginary.

I wish to express my thanks to the Friends of the Joseph Schneider Haus and to Susan Burke, Manager-Curator of the Joseph Schneider Haus Museum, along with Katherine McCracken, Curatorial Assistant; Cathy Blackbourn, Education Coordinator; Karen Rennie, Teacher-Programmer; Anne-Marie Bettschen, Clerk; Kathryn Plunkett, Teacher-Interpreter; Michelle Spencer, Teacher-Interpreter; Mara Hollands, Teacher-Interpreter; Drew Maxwell, Weekend Interpreter; Steve Mavers, Weekend Supervisor; and Junior Interpreters Charlene Arbor, Nadine Borch, Laura Sauder, Kim Snyder, and Katherine Vernelli; as well as Nancy Martin and Matthias Martin, Miriam Sokvitne, Linda Schryer, Sandra Woolfrey, Evie Hill, Elizabeth Morley, and Paul Tiessen for their help, advice, and encouragement in the writing of this book. I also wish to acknowledge Gisela Brude-Firnau and Nancy Martin for their translations from the Eby *ABC* and the *Lieder-Sammlung*; I have added metre and rhyme. My thanks, as always, go first and last to my husband and fellow scholar, E Palmer Patterson.

Nancy-Lou Patterson

About the Author

In *The Tramp Room*, Nancy-Lou Patterson (Distinguished Emerita Professor of Fine Arts, University of Waterloo, and D.Litt., honoris causa, Wilfrid Laurier University) brings together her skills as scholar and author. Of her many scholarly works, *Mennonite Traditional Art* (1979), *Wreath and Bough* (1983) and *The Language of Paradise* (1985), and some sixty articles are devoted to Mennonite culture. Her previous works for young adult readers include *Apple Staff and Silver Crown* (1985), *The Painted Hallway* (1992) and *Barricade Summer* (1996). Based on careful research and deep empathy for the communities she portrays, *The Tramp Room* is a major milestone in her creative career.

Nancy-Lou Patterson, artist, poet, scholar and author, says, "For four decades I combined university teaching with mothering nine children and publishing scholarly articles and books." In her young-adult novels, she combines a historian's accuracy, an artist's vision and a poet's voice.

Table of Contents

Chapter One: St. Nicholas Eve 1

Chapter Two: The Tramp Boy 9

Chapter Three: Visitors 19

Chapter Four: Flax Breaking 29

Chapter Five: The Bushlot 39

Chapter Six: Sausage Making 47

Chapter Seven: The Lamb's Table 57

Chapter Eight: A Snowstorm 69

Chapter Nine: Goose Quills 79

Chapter Ten: Candle Making 89

Chapter Eleven: The Spinning Room 99

Chapter Twelve: Peace Cookies 109

Chapter Thirteen: More Visitors 121

Chapter Fourteen: *Christkindl* 131

Chapter Fifteen: St. Nicholas Day 141

Chapter One: St. Nicholas Eve

"**C**an I stay overnight with my friend Malinda afterwards?" I asked Mama.

Every December as long as I could remember, my mother, Professor Tessa Salisbury, had brought me and my little brothers to the St. Nicholas Eve Reception at the Joseph Schneider Haus Museum, the restored Mennonite house in the Waterloo Region.

"I suppose so, Elizabeth. How will you get to school tomorrow?" Mama asked. She had to give a talk later on in the evening, and needed to arrange my transportation first.

I had come to spend that evening wearing nineteenth-century costume, because I was a junior interpreter for the museum, and would play the part of a cousin of the family that had built the house so long ago. Mama and I were sitting in the kitchen, where everything was furnished as it would have been a hundred and fifty years ago when the Joseph Schneider family had lived there. The candle flames on the kitchen table cast light over the brightly glazed earthenware plates piled with holiday cookies, and their doubles reflected from the windowpanes that looked out of the side and front of the house.

"Malinda's mother can take me," I answered, and Mama agreed. After she and my brothers went out, one of the adult interpreters came in, also in costume. "This is our storyteller," she said, waving at a young woman beside her. "She's come to entertain the children while the adults hear your mother's talk."

"Shall I show you the room where you'll read?" I asked.

The storyteller nodded, and, taking up a candle, I led her to the base of a steep flight of stairs climbing up the side wall of the kitchen.

"Up here," I said, taking hold of the bannister with one hand and lifting the candle with the other, so she could see her way. "That's the spare bedroom," I told her, when we reached the top.

"Oh."

"And that's the boys' room," I added. "In the corner."

"Mm."

"And this is the beggar's room. Some people call it the tramp room." I held up the candle to show her the narrow, windowless room next to the boys' room.

"The tramp room?" she asked, beginning to sound interested.

"Yes. A room for travellers. Men who were looking for work back in the early 1850s. Craftsmakers moving from job to job. The family who lived here let them sleep in it." I had been taught what to say when taking people through the house.

"Oh," she said. "Like the monks in the Middle Ages, who gave rooms to visitors. 'Let every guest be received as Christ.'"

I peered into the dark space, furnished by a bed no wider than a man's body, half the size of a usual single bed.

"I suppose so." I followed her as she moved past me, feeling a sudden shiver at having that cramped and empty room behind my back.

"Here's the spinning room." I had moved on to the end of the hall, where the street lights in front of the house shone between the two tall evergreens.

"And this is the room where the daughters of the Schneider family slept. It's where we usually have our storytelling." My candle shot light into the open space, showing a series of warmly covered beds.

"I'll sit here," the storyteller said. She strode in and sat down on a stool directly in front of the big wardrobe, with her back to it.

At exactly that moment, we heard the sound of many feet coming upstairs, and the adult interpreter led a crowd of mothers and their children along the hall to the door of the girls' room. The children pushed in and sat themselves down in a semicircle in front of the storyteller, and most of the mothers went back downstairs to hear the talks.

I slid past the seated children to the end of the room farthest from the door, and sat down too, on the floor. I set my candle on a little table between the farthest bed and the end wall, and waited for the story to begin, but I never found out how it ended. I lay down and listened, curled with my cheek in the curve of my arm, warm in my winter costume. The children's voices and the storyteller's tale slowly sank away into nothingness.

Afterwards, how long I couldn't tell, I awakened, and pushed myself up from where I lay, until I sat with my feet stretched out and my body stiff and sore. All I could hear was a sound like quiet breathing, as if nearly every bed in the room had somebody in it, sound asleep. Then I recognized the soft hiss of rain, stood up, and looked out a window into the night.

As far as I could see, the earth reached away flat and wet under a dark, low-hanging sky. The street lights must have gone off while I slept, I thought. Then, with a start, I remembered something; I had forgotten to ask Malinda for a ride.

I jumped up, my heart pounding. No candles burned anywhere. I must have outslept them. How could I have been so stupid? And Mama—Mama must have gone home trustfully without me. I shook my head, little tears of panic and frustration spilling on my cheeks.

"Mercy," I whispered between clenched teeth, saying what Mama would have said.

Then I froze. Somebody—or something—gave a girlish sigh from one of the beds, and I heard the soft but distinct sound of a young body turning under a load of coverings. Carefully I put my hand out to the bed beside me, and touched a woollen coverlet, its prickles clearly announcing themselves to my fingertips.

What made me snatch my hand away was not the rough wool, but the warmth of that bed. Clearly, somebody alive lay there breathing peacefully; somebody, I felt sure, that I did not know.

I stood perfectly still. Each of the beds had occupants, I realized, all sleeping soundly. Had some of the storyteller's listeners crept into these beds and fallen asleep? I went carefully, step-by-step, terrified of finding a creaking floorboard, to where the door stood, according to my feeling fingers, only just not quite shut. Carefully, I pushed it open and slipped out into the hall.

Here too a window let the faintest light into the interior, but when I looked away back along the hall toward the rear of the house, my gaze met only darkness, so deep I hated to turn my back on it again.

Nothing down there but the boys' room and the tramp room, and the spare room, I told myself. That was the problem; all those rooms, and each as empty as the other. Unless, I suddenly thought, they weren't empty. Maybe they had sleeping people in them too!

This mad idea made me press myself against the windowsill as if I could somehow get out that way, when a sudden sound froze me in my place.

Bam. Bam. The knocking sounded like thunder in the upstairs stillness. It wasn't a loud sound, really; but it came again and again, a distant, sharp rapping of knuckles with no mitts or gloves in the way. Somebody stood on the veranda at the door below, the big six-panelled front door that opened directly into the kitchen, and knocked.

In a moment I heard movement downstairs, a whispering shuffle in the dark that echoed upstairs and along the hall; someone up and awake, moving from the back part of the house. I remembered then the large bedroom at the rear of the main floor where the parents of the family which had once lived in the house had slept in their big four-poster bed, with their littlest children in the cradle and the trundle bed there.

The footsteps, in all the silent, downstairs darkness, moved clearly below me through the kitchen, and toward the front door. Pulled by a sharp curiosity, I tiptoed along my upstairs hallway, through its pressing shadows to the head of the stairs, and looked down.

I couldn't see much of the door from up there, because another stairway led from the upper floor to the attic overhead, its slanted back blocking my view. But I could see light, increasing as the soft footsteps came toward where I knew the front door had to be.

Then, almost unexpectedly, a figure appeared. A slender woman padded forward on bare feet, wearing a white linen nightgown and draped in a shawl, with her hair tucked up under her nightcap.

She stopped for a moment exactly at the foot of the stairway as if she might turn and come up, and then, while my heartbeat raced, she moved forward purposefully, just beyond my sight, and—from the protesting sound of its hinges and the sweep of cold air up the stairway—opened the door.

A moment later, a young boy stepped indoors and into my sight. I couldn't see his face clearly, but I could make out his silhouette against the faint blue light that must have shone through the doorway still opened behind him. The woman's form moved between the boy and me, but his image, young, slender, and hesitant, entered my memory and stayed there, never to be forgotten.

Before I could fully understand what I had seen, the shape of a tall, dark-bearded man moved into the room and passed beyond the woman. Then, by the sound of it, he closed and locked the big door.

A sudden flow of light burst out as a candle, lifted by the woman—the mother, as I knew she must be, cast its beam over the boy, and I caught a glimpse of his pale face and his dark hair falling in loose curls over his forehead, as he stood there, clutching something dark and rolled up against his chest.

The people spoke to him, their voices kept low as if not wanting to wake the children; I understood then that there were many children in the house, asleep in their rooms. With a quick gesture, the mother pulled off her shawl and draped it around the boy's shoulders.

"Come up," she whispered, and even as I recognized her German dialect, I understood it, somehow.

They began to mount the stairs; I shrank back, afraid of being heard retreating. Moving backwards a step at a time, I slipped into the spare bedroom and stood there in darkness, forgetting the emptiness at my back, trembling not only with fear but with curiosity, as the mother and father and the boy came slowly up. He moved like a person at the end of his strength, step after step, so slender his weight scarcely brought out a sound from the well-scrubbed treads, still holding whatever it was that he had in his arms, while the parents of the household creaked up behind him.

Nobody glanced into the place where I stood, and I watched, hoping they wouldn't hear the pounding of my heart, holding my breath as they passed.

"Here," the mother whispered, "Here's a room for you."

She had stopped in front of the open-doored tramp room, that dark, cramped slot with its sliver-thin bed. I all but cried out; not there! She laid a hand on his shoulder, and I saw him wince, but he walked in, leaned over the bed to put down his burden, and stood obediently with his back to us all.

He began to take off his clothes; the mother's shawl first, then a sodden shirt, which he pulled over his head. As the shirt-tail moved up his back, I saw his spine, every knob casting a shadow in the candlelight, and his shoulder blades poking through his skin as if he were halfway starving. Then, as he drew his shirt completely away, I saw that his shoulders were badly bruised.

I must have gasped; the mother whirled around and thrust the candle toward me, as I stood just inside the spare bedroom.

"You're here?" she asked, surprised but not shocked. "Good. We have a guest, and he's drenched to the bone. I'll get him a dry shirt to sleep in, and you can bring a comforter; there's one in the storage chest. Quick, now, that's a good girl."

I spun around and walked deeper into the room, heading across its darkness to where I expected to find a big painted chest, squatting low and protective, full of homespun linen and wool-stuffed comforters, laid inside for safekeeping. I felt its presence in the dark with my body, first, before my outstretched fingers touched it, and I raised its heavy lid, smelling the breath of pine-wood and lanolin. I filled my arms with a thick comforter, the first thing to meet my fingertips.

"Here!" I staggered with it to where the mother stood outside the tramp-room door.

She had given the candle to the father, who waited, a tall, still presence, beside her. In a single gesture she took it from me, flung it out full length, and swung it over the shivering body of the boy as he lay curled up on the narrow bed. Then she left him, in the dry, long-tailed shirt they had put on him, under the comforter that hid him like a mound of sheltering snow.

Chapter Two: The Tramp Boy

I woke early, to find a fat woollen comforter pressing me into a mattress that sagged on the cross-laced ropes of a low wooden bedstead. When I tried to roll over, the heavy linen sheets felt like canvas, and when I lifted my head from my deep feather pillow, I could see that all the other beds still held sleepers, with their heads covered in linen nightcaps.

I sat up to meet the early morning chill of the room and a shudder reminded me that the fire in the stove downstairs must have been banked down to smouldering coals, just enough to start again in the morning. And this was, I could now see, only just morning, a heartbeat after dawn.

But I had to know. I put my bare feet carefully onto the icy cold, smoothly painted wooden floor. In a moment I had reached the window, gritting my teeth so they wouldn't chatter, and I looked out into a world I had never seen. Beyond the grassy yard, on the other side of the white picket fence, a muddy, rutted country road went by, and beyond that, a farmer's field began, exactly at the spot where last night there had been a parking lot. In the distance, I could see trees, orange and copper and gold, all bright with autumn, as the sun coming up beyond their rain-washed leaves set them alight.

Trembling, I tiptoed away from the window, along the hall toward the top of the stairs. The tramp-room door had been closed, something I had never seen before, but the boys'-room door stood ajar. As quietly as I could, I peeped in. I saw the horizontal opening, like a window frame with no windowpanes, that let some light and air into the tramp room through its side wall. The beds had been slept in; their covers lay rumpled, pulled back from the empty sheets.

As I stood still, I realized that I knew very well whose room this must be. The brothers, of course, of the four sisters who slept in the room I had just left. And I knew exactly who they were; I'd even seen a family photograph of them, all grown up, some with grey hair, taken in the first decade of the twentieth century; the children of Joseph and Sarah Schneider.

A flash of dizzy nausea made me grab the doorpost; reality lurched and slipped, as if the whole earth had given itself a shake while I stood there trying to hold on.

11

Could I, I asked myself while I began to recover, could I actually be in the nineteenth century? Really and truly, in the time where I had been pretending to be, with my historic costume, the one I had slept in and was still wearing; the time I had been taught about so I could explain things to visitors when they came to explore the Joseph Schneider Haus?

I backed away from the boys'-room door, almost bumping into the bannister above the stairs, and moved as quietly as I could to the head of the staircase where I had stood the night before. I remembered it all, and now I knew when it had happened; in the mid-1850s, when these children had been, and now were, young. Time had turned inside out, I thought, and had taken me with it, though I didn't know how or why.

Just as I accepted this impossible fact, I heard a sound downstairs. Bracing myself for whatever I would find, I put a foot on the topmost step, and then, ever so carefully, began to walk down, at least far enough to peek over the bannister.

And there he was; the boy I had seen the night before. He sat on a small chair in front of the big black stove, with his feet drawn up. I could see his thin shoulders and his dark tousled hair as he sat with his back to me. He had wrapped his comforter around himself; he looked very small as I gazed down at the top of his head.

I moved slowly down the last steps, and he must have heard me, for he turned his head to look up. As he did, a flash of light shot across his face from the window; the sun had peeped above the distant treetops, and now poured into the kitchen. His hair shone suddenly around his head like a flare, and his face, pale and pinched as it was, looked up at me like a flower, open and aware.

"Good morning," he said, in a different form of German than the dialect the mother had used the night before, and he rose up from the chair.

"Good morning!" I answered, and I must have been speaking German too, though I didn't know how or why I could.

I stepped down from the last of the stairs, and as I turned toward him, he waited with his bare feet planted firmly on the painted floor. Face to face, he stood as tall as I did, no child, but a young teenager near my own age. He looked directly into my eyes in a way nobody ever did before or after, and I experienced a feeling of being recognized and remembered, of being known, really known, exactly as myself and no other.

Then he held out his hand, with its unexpectedly strong fingers, calloused from some sort of very hard work, and before I could think about it, I held out my own hand, and our fingers touched in a quick handclasp. As I slowly pulled my fingers away, I saw a silver scar in the palm of his hand.

"What happened?" I asked.

"A careless chisel," he said.

"What were you doing with the chisel?"

His face, which had been open and bright, began to close.

"Where did you work?" I asked, hoping to see him smile again.

"With a cabinetmaker," he answered, in a low voice. "At least, that's what he said himself to be."

"Where was this?"

"In Pennsylvania."

Of course, I thought, many German craftsworkers had come— no, I corrected myself, had come and would come—to Waterloo County, drawn by the German-speaking Mennonite community who had come before them.

"So you came here from Pennsylvania with the man you apprenticed to?"

"No."

"You came alone?"

He said nothing, but I went on anyway.

"Had you finished your contract with him, then? What became of your new suit—your freedom clothes—and all the other things you were supposed to get when you completed your work?"

I remembered what I had been taught about the apprentice system when the museum had shown an exhibition of historic furniture.

A faint smile, so narrow I could hardly believe I saw the same person, flickered at the corner of his mouth. "No, I didn't finish my contract, if you could call it a contract."

"You ran away from your obligation?"

He gave me a level look. "Not exactly. But I'm on my own, all the same."

"Does he know where you are?"

"I hope not."

Before I could think of another way to ask him what had happened, little feet came scampering into the kitchen, not from the stairs, but through the pantry at the back of the house that led to a storeroom and into the main floor's corner bedroom. A small girl appeared, dressed in a linen nightgown and cap and hugging a homemade toy—a dog, all floppy ears and curled tail made of grey ticking—followed by the woman who had approached me last night, Sarah Schneider.

"Up already?" she asked me. "And you haven't filled the stove? The wood's on the side porch." Then, to the child, she added, "We have company, Lena!"

As soon as she spoke, the boy trotted, barefoot as he was, out the side door of the kitchen, and I followed him to find the wood stacked in a neat pile. He filled his arms with split firewood, while I gathered up kindling; those arms, though thin, were muscular with a craftsman's lean and accurate strength.

As we came inside, I looked closely at the stove. Made of black iron, it rose majestically from splayed animal feet, bellied out to support a broad, flat surface, then reached up to a flue which heated a large oven, shaped like a barrel lying on its side, and then pushed still further up and through the ceiling. Its large, well-polished presence began to radiate warmth as the wood put in by the mother flamed up from its bed of slumbering coals.

"What's your trade, lad?" Sarah asked the boy, so unexpectedly that it made me jump.

Rattled, I answered for him. "He's a cabinetmaker."

He looked at her with wary eyes, his face guarded and still.

"A tramp, are you? On the road?"

"Yes."

"Looking for work?"

"If I can find it."

"You may be in luck then," she said, in a voice so gentle I felt a tug of longing. "I'll see if Joseph can use an extra hand in getting everything done before the snow flies."

"Thank you." A hint of his earlier brightness flashed across his face.

"You can stay in the tramp room, then."

The minute her mother said this, little Magdalene, who had been called "Lena" by her mother, reached up to the boy, and he lifted her, along with her toy dog, onto the curve of his arm, and began to dance around the kitchen table, with his passenger squealing for joy. Within moments, footsteps slapped down the stairs from above.

"See if the kettle's boiling," Sarah said to me, as the other daughters began to appear. "We want it hot when Father and the boys come in from their chores."

The girls, all showing signs of having dressed hastily, giggled at the sight of the boy with their little sister on his arm, prancing about in his bare feet, and he stopped, looking shy, and put the child down gently.

"You are a tramp?" the tallest and oldest girl asked. I knew she must be Barbara; she looked more like a young woman than a girl.

"What else could he be?" asked a girl I guessed was her next youngest sister, Mary.

Then they all had something to say. He answered them each with a few mild, guarded words, his face alert, and his eyes seeming to read them, searching past their faces to their minds inside.

The girls began to set the table, and the tramp boy went out to fetch water for the dry sink and to bring in extra wood, at their mother's direction. I tried to help out as I saw the girls doing, and found that most of what I did was right.

"Get the baby, would you?" Sarah asked me. "She'll be jumping out of her cradle by now." I realized that the littlest child, baby Sarah, must be still in her parents' bedroom, and I went through the pantry and the storage room beyond it, to the bedroom door. Pushing the door open carefully, I tiptoed in, hoping not to wake the baby if she was still asleep.

Then I heard giggles, almost ready to become whines, and I hurried to pick her up, her cheeks smelling of milk, and her little rosebud mouth making milky bubbles. She cuddled against me and I carried her warm, and, as I was beginning to realize, damp, into the kitchen, snatching down a cloth that I now recognized as a child's diaper from a wooden peg in the storage room.

"Look who's here," I announced as I came back to the kitchen, and the sisters took tiny Sarah away from me, each eager for a turn.

When the table had been completely set and the kettle had boiled, and the food stood steaming in great earthenware bowls, Joseph Schneider came stamping up onto the side porch in his heavy boots, changed them for indoor shoes he had left there, and entered the kitchen still breathing steam for a second or two past the door, smiling at his assembled daughters. Behind him came his two sons, David and Samuel, both stamping as their father had done.

One after another they entered, paused, and looked to see what they could see.

Their father's eyes rested upon the face of the tramp boy, who, at the sight of him, began almost visibly to shrink, clenching his fists and staring at the floor, while his face grew pale and his lips pinched. I could almost feel him trembling from across the room.

"So, here's our visitor," Joseph said, his voice mild and low. "Come and let me see you in the daylight."

"Yes, sir," he whispered.

The father put out his hand, and, carefully, the boy extended his own, and they shook hands.

"You've done hard work, I can see that," Joseph told him. "Would you like to work for me, for a while? Just until you get on your feet, of course." His eyes and those of his wife met over the boy's head, and they smiled agreement.

"With all my heart," the tramp boy answered.

Sarah began to ladle cornmeal porridge into everybody's bowls, and, after a blessing, she began the task of carefully cutting and handing around the table the big brown-crusted pies. The boys helped themselves to large spoonfuls of boiled and sugared dried apples and dried pears passing the big bowls that took two hands to move them from place to place. Their mother poured coffee and milk into earthenware cups and these, too, were passed around the table from place to place.

At last, taking the baby onto her lap, she sat down.

After that, nobody said a word. They ate and drank as if they had never eaten before and would never eat again. After all, the boys and their father had been up before the sun, seeing to their chores, and the rest of us had arisen at sunrise, prepared the food, and set it on the table. The tramp boy, more than anybody, attended to his eating, putting his spoon into his mouth in quick, silent motions, staring at his plate and cup as if he thought that food and drink alike might disappear if he glanced away, even for a second.

Chapter Three: Visitors

The rest of the day seemed to last forever, as the girls and their mother and I worked in the kitchen and in the smokehouse with its big bake oven, cooking and baking for the weekend to follow. We had to do this in advance because unnecessary work was not supposed to be done on Sunday. We made twenty-four pies, and ten huge loaves of bread, and several dozen buns. The mixing, rolling, baking, setting out to cool, and putting away in the pantry went on until I thought that a whole church full of people must be expected, and I wasn't far wrong.

The day after that was just as long. We scarcely saw our tramp boy because he went out before the light came, along with the two Schneider sons and their father. I caught a glimpse of him once, when I had been sent to bring in more eggs; the henhouse, like the smokehouse and other outbuildings, stood behind the house. I had the eggs, brown and speckled, with flecks of straw stuck to them, in an old, worn basket, and, seeing him, I stopped.

Dressed, now, exactly as the other two boys were, he looked right at home, except for his pale cheeks, and even these were just beginning to change. Anybody who didn't know us would have thought they saw a nineteenth-century Mennonite, hired girl and hired boy, stopping for a chat as they went about their chores.

"Have you worked here long?" he asked me. Something in the way I acted must have told him that I, like him, was not quite part of the family.

"Not long," I answered.

"But they've been good to you." He said this as a statement, not a question.

"Oh, yes," I replied, and I meant it.

He smiled again, and then walked away, back to his work. I stood still, watching him; he already moved differently, less defensively, less like a person who thought he might get a smack at any moment.

That night, everybody bathed. The older brother, David, and his father took turns pumping water from the backyard pump into buckets, and carrying them with more than a few splashes along the side porch, hefting them onto the kitchen stove, which the younger brother, Samuel, kept heated, putting in stick after stick of wood that the tramp boy had carried in before going outside to get more.

When the water had become hot but not boiling—Sarah dipped her elbow in to make sure—everybody washed and washed, or at least I certainly did, until we were bright red all over from scrubbing ourselves, and our hair squeaked wetly in our combs. Sarah found me the comb I used, and gave me a cloth bag to put it in afterwards.

"This was mine, when I was a girl," she said. "See my initials?"

The tiny letters had been neatly embroidered in cross-stitch, in a red thread on the white linen bag that could be closed with a drawstring and hung from a bedpost.

"Thank you," I said. "I'm glad to have it."

After she had washed the two little girls, she had laid them down to sleep in the trundle bed and the cradle in the downstairs bedroom. Now she waited upstairs with us, as we dressed in our nightclothes and caps, said our prayers, and went to bed. I wondered then and for several more nights until I gave up hoping, whether I might wake up in the morning in my own century. But things didn't go exactly like that.

Instead, I woke up where—and when—I had been the night before. After eating breakfast, Sarah said to me, "Get the little ones ready for church, and yourself too," taking it for granted that I must be a Mennonite.

Joseph brought the carriage, drawn by his two huge work-horses, around to the side of the house, with the two brothers in it, and gave us each a hand up; his wife in front, and the sisters and me in the back with the babies in our laps. The tramp boy stood last in line with an expression on his face like a person who didn't know exactly what to do.

I saw Joseph and Sarah glance at each other, wondering, I thought, whether they should take him, and not wanting to impose upon him if he didn't want to go. Maybe they knew from the way he spoke German that he wasn't part of their community. Whatever they thought, in the end, he didn't come with us.

Instead, the mother said to him, softly, "See how many eggs you can find while we're gone, and I'll cook egg cheese for you when we get back. There's some maple syrup yet, enough to make it sweet. Would you like that?"

Then away we went to the Mennonite Meeting House, where the women sat on one side and the men on the other, and the sermons were, at least from my point of view, very, very long. Nothing lasts forever, and the teaching of godliness and peace never hurt anybody, I told myself. Besides, I had never heard such singing; the whole congregation sang together without either choir or organ, or any other musical instrument.

Afterwards, we all drove out along the road again with everybody sitting up straight and able to enjoy the view as we made our way home. When we got there, we found the tramp boy waiting in the kitchen. He held out a delicate basket, filled to the top with fat brown eggs, and presented it to the mother after she had hung her big, fringed shawl on a peg near the stove.

"You've found a new basket as well as fresh eggs, have you?" she asked, looking closely at the neat, little coiled basket, shaped like a nest, that he held out to her on his two cupped hands.

"I made it," he said.

"Did your master teach you how?" she asked. "This is a well-made thing."

"No. My mother taught me." A flash of pain glinted in his eyes.

"Well, I thank you," she said, and put the basket of eggs in the pantry. Meanwhile the girls had gone upstairs, coming down with aprons and indoor caps, ready to help set out the Sunday meal. As this work proceeded, they took turns running out onto the veranda and gazing along the road to see if any buggies were in sight and would soon arrive.

"Go into the sitting room—here's a dustcloth—and make sure to find all the dust!" the mother said to me. Until that moment, I hadn't seen a single soul in that family enter the big room that opened from the kitchen at the foot of the stairs. I felt honoured to be allowed inside it alone, and went in carefully, looking for any dust that might still be hiding where somebody had obviously dusted already.

In the middle of that carefully set aside space, I stopped, and turned slowly around. Unlike the warm and welcoming kitchen, with its lower walls of deep earth-coloured red, and its floor of yellow ochre, the walls in the sitting room were pale grey, like a pigeon's outspread wing, with a deeper grey rail all around, just at the height of the windowsills. The light curtains of precious printed cloth were pulled apart and held open by painted pegs. The handmade glass of the windows made the out-of-doors waver and bend, but the light coming in showed that every pane had been washed for company.

Most of the tall, handsome furniture, gracefully made and carefully polished, stood against the four walls. The floor of dark ochre shone too, and had no rugs. Many chairs, large and small, stood along the walls, waiting for the company to arrive. A small black woodstove, whose chimney went up through the girls' room on its way to the roof, gave off a pleasant warmth, ready to greet our visitors.

A single door connected the sitting room to the parents' bedroom; of course it was kept closed most of the time. It had a purpose, however, beyond that of protecting their privacy. On its grey surface, a wonderful linen towel, more than an arm's length long, hung proudly, displayed in a room which had no paintings or other wall decorations.

This towel had been formed from a series of pieces of linen, and each piece had been attached to the one above it, so that a set of fringes marked the beginning of each new section, from top to bottom, where the longest fringe of all had been formed into a row of neat tassels. Each of the sections had been beautifully embroidered with cross-stitch designs in red and blue thread on the snowy white linen.

I saw Trees of Life, Paradise trees full of birds and flowers, arranged with a big tree in the centre and smaller trees set one on each side. Every panel looked like a magical garden, with some trees growing from baskets, and some from what looked like water vessels, too big to be vases, with large handles. In every tree, pairs of birds perched on the branches, and on some trees, single birds perched on the topmost bough.

On one of the upper panels, I found the mother's name, not her married name, but her maiden name, in elaborate letters, and above that, a row of hearts and crowns and little sprays of flowers that looked like tulips and carnations. I knew that she must have made this beautiful example of her skills as a needleworker when she, too, was a very young teenager, just like me.

Suddenly, I heard a mechanical grinding, as of many wheels and sprockets. I spun around and saw, standing on the floor in front of the opposite wall, the tall grandfather clock. It had wakened in its dark cabinet, its face painted with roses and garlands, and, with a wheeze and a creak it began to chime, the deep tone announcing the time for Sunday dinner. That sent me scampering to finish my work, and I hurried to the big desk, carefully passing my dustcloth over its many panels, and, in spite of my haste, prying open its desktop and peeking inside to see the many small drawers and doors and storage slots inside.

I had only just finished my dusting when the first steps sounded on the side porch outside the kitchen, and the first knocks rattled the side door. I hurried back into the kitchen to be met by family after family, all seeming to come at once. With cheerful greetings and shaken hands, and whoops from some of the younger boys, and squeals from the younger girls, hangings up of shawls and coats and hats on the many pegs, hugs exchanged and hands shaken, the men gathered in the sitting room and the women in the kitchen, until the dinner was ready to be served.

Only after we had all eaten everything—the pies and the rolls and the bread, the pats of sweet butter shaped like flowers or pineapples or birds, the slices of meat, the bowls of vegetables, the seven kinds of sweet dishes and the seven kinds of sour pickles, the pitchers of raspberry vinegar diluted with water—did I realize that the tramp boy had not joined us. Maybe, I reasoned, he was afraid to be seen.

Then, as I helped to clear away what remained of the feast, and the many dishes that needed to be washed, I saw on a shelf in the pantry a bowl and a cup, with a knife and fork and spoon, as if, in all the excitement, he had eaten alone and washed up for himself.

The mother, seeing me look at these forlorn things, when she came in behind me to put something away, spoke softly.

"He's a shy one," she said.

"Yes."

One of the younger girls, Lydia, who had followed her mother in, tugged at my elbow. "Come on! We're all going upstairs," she told me, and, as the mother gave me permission to go, with a nod and a smile, I followed the child upstairs, leaning over to tie her apron for her as we went.

Mounting the stairs, I could hear the voices of the visitors, chatting and laughing in the sitting room, and the footsteps of the other girls ahead of us, already in the hall above, on their way to the bedroom where I and the Schneider sisters slept. When I came along with little Lydia, every bed had girls sitting on it, and some had found places on the floor as well, where I joined them.

They spent most of the afternoon talking weddings. Our Barbara, soon to be married, with only two years to wait—the usual time for planning a wedding—and having everything in readiness for the new household, introduced the subject, and everybody joined in.

"I'll have three bedsteads in my dowry," she said as we listened attentively, "and bedding for all three. I'll show you what I've made so far; all hemmed and embroidered with my initials."

The smaller girls breathed in chorus, "Ah!"

"And I'll have a kitchen cupboard, and a dry sink with a copper lining."

I thought of the wooden cupboard in the kitchen downstairs, full of earthenware bowls and plates and cups, and the wooden sink, to which one had to bring water in a bucket from the well; water that, when drained out of a square-shaped wooden pipe through the wall of the house, fell onto the ground. Dishes were washed in a basin placed in that sink; they were always carefully scraped first to get the last scraps of food for the pigs.

"And two drop-leaf tables, one small and one large," the big sister continued, breaking into my thoughts, "and six kitchen chairs."

Everybody sighed, imagining this wonderful furniture, polished and new.

"Will the table have a drawer with carved handles?" one of the girl guests asked.

"Of course! And I'll have a waterfall-seat rocking chair, too." That meant the chair seat would have a curved front edge.

"Mm," we answered, approvingly.

"Three metal washtubs."

"Ah!"

"A butter churn, and a baking trough."

These last items, remainders of the long tasks of churning, endlessly lifting up and down the wooden dasher, and of kneading bread and letting it rise over and over, left everybody silent, thinking, maybe, about all the tasks and chores, and other everyday sides of marriage.

"And, of course," she added, "a nice china chamber pot, and a washstand with its pitcher and bowl made of china."

"Of course," we all agreed.

"And a sideboard, and good china dishes. With the railroad coming in soon, I'll have no more earthenware."

We began to talk about railroads, but she cut us short. "And I'll have a big storage chest, full of linens and woollens, and as many feather ticks as I need."

"Mama will let you pluck the geese," small Magdalene said, and everybody laughed, until she hung her head and put out her lip, and had to be hugged and reassured.

"You're right," Barbara smiled. "or maybe I'll have my own geese and can pluck them instead."

"Now, then," one of the visitors asked, catching this lull in the conversation, "who's that boy, the one that's visiting here?"

I sat perfectly still, as if frozen, though she hadn't spoken to me.

"Just a tramp boy," the next oldest sister, Mary, told her. "They come by all the time. It's because we're so near the town."

"Yes," Barbara added, with her hands lying quietly in her lap. "We've had a great many tramps, but we've never yet found a bed-bug!"

They all laughed, hearing this familiar joke, and passed on to other things. But I had been scared, made aware of how vulnerable our tramp boy was, living among people who would all, as the weeks went by, visit one another and know each family's business as well as they knew their own.

Later, when the company had gone, we straightened out the chairs, and swept and dusted the room again. Joseph Schneider wound the clock; I knew he must have done this regularly since it had come into his household.

We ate a quiet supper of the leftovers, meat chopped and refried with some of the morning's corn porridge, and the last of the pies. Sarah Schneider, true to her word, made egg cheese, using the eggs the tramp boy had gathered for her, along with sour milk and sugar, and set it to cool in the pantry with a cloth on top.

"I know today is Sunday," she said, when she saw Barbara looking surprised, "but this isn't non-essential work. It's lawful to do a good deed on the Sabbath."

Bringing it to the table, she poured last-of-the season maple syrup over it, and the sharp, sweet, smoky taste of it lingered on my tongue after supper. She served the tramp boy first, because, as she said, he had made a basket for the family. He ate every speck, and licked his spoon afterwards until the last bit of sweetness had gone. Eating was a serious business to him, I realized; he could never be sure if he would eat like that again.

When he finished, he raised his dark eyes to her, and smiled, as suddenly and brightly as on that first morning when I had found him alone in the kitchen.

Chapter Four: Flax Breaking

Gradually, the tramp boy and I both settled into the household, finding our way around by watching the others, and by doing as we were told. Not that we were often together. Over time, I became familiar with the family, and knew how old they were, and what sort of person each one of them was.

Joseph Schneider had dark hair on his head, and a dark beard on his chin. His brown eyes shone when he looked at his wife, Sarah, slim and fair-haired, with a pink complexion and bright blue eyes. They worked together as a team, though their work—his in the barn and fields, and hers in the house and garden—kept them apart for much of the day.

Their eldest daughter, Barbara, a handsome young woman of eighteen, looked like her mother, and so did one of the younger sisters, Lydia, whom I knew to be seven or so; both shared their mother's fair hair and colouring. Between Barbara and Mary, who was twelve, came the two boys, both the image of their father. The older boy, David, a tall, lanky sixteen, carried himself as if he knew everything, and his worshipful younger brother, Samuel, who followed him like a shadow, hadn't yet reached his full growth at fourteen, and feared, I suppose, that he never would.

Between the two blonde daughters were two sisters, dark like their father. At twelve, the elder of these, Mary, had left school to help out at home, but the nine-year-old Louisa, along with her fair, younger sister, Lydia still went to school, wrapped up in shawls and bonnets, with me as an escort to see that they didn't dawdle at the roadside or fall into the creek.

"With so many new folk coming into town," their mother told me, "it can't hurt to have an eye on them." And when I got back each day, there to be played with between chores were the little ones, the busy five-year-old Magdalene and baby Sarah, just turned two, whose dark curls resembled those of her father.

As for me, I had always been fair-haired and blue-eyed; tucked in among the children of the Schneider household, who called me "Lizbet," I suppose I looked as much like most of them as could be expected. Certainly, I never had time to brood or worry. Everybody on the farm had plenty to do.

31

"Lucky we had an extra bed frame that just fits at the end of the room," Sarah said to me one day not long after I had arrived. "We never used it before you came to us." We laced the ropes to hold up the straw mattress, which we filled with golden, sweet-smelling straw that reminded me of summer every time I went to bed. I always fell asleep without having to think about it, glad to lie down after the long busy days with cool air and bright sunlight outside, and plenty of things to do indoors, too.

The tramp boy spent most of his time with the brothers and their father, busy getting every last growing thing stored away in one or another of the barn's great mows, or storage bins, set one storey above the other. His cheeks began to show colour, half from October sunlight, and half from chapping on cold mornings. They had lost their hollows, and had rounded out. I knew that if I caught him again without his shirt, his bones would be hidden away behind his skin again, from three good meals a day and regular work among people who needed his help.

"Come along," I heard Sarah calling, as I came back one day from taking Louisa and Lydia to school, and found her draping the damp dishcloths over the rack hung high above the stove. "You can help us ready the flax for spinning." Then, turning to Mary, she added, "See if your father can spare our tramp boy; he can turn his hand to breaking or scutching. He's patient and careful enough to do such work."

"I'll get him," I said, "and I know how to scutch. I can hackle, too."

"Your mother's been a good teacher."

"Yes," I said, feeling a pang of memory. As a young interpreter, I had been taught how to prepare flax for spinning. I draped my shawl over my shoulders, pulled my cap strings tight, and trotted out along the side porch, and then walked to the south, toward the tall bank barn.

It reared its great bulk up, sheltering both animals and stored crops under its huge roof. The lower stable level, set into its earthen bank, protected the pigs and cows and horses, and in the winter, the sheep. The upper level, a wooden threshing floor, held the first set of mows and granaries where the straw and grain were stored. Above these a second set of mows made room for even more, and above all this, the tall bents or braces formed of long posts and crosspieces, reached up to support the rafters, which held the roof. Slim shafts of light fell from slotted windows, and pigeons fluttered and warbled up there, in a world of their own. The whole complex assembly of wooden parts was held together by pegs, as each piece fitted into the next by a short extension into a shallow slot.

This, too, reminded me of Mama, who had written a book about barns and taken me along, when I was little, as she went around the countryside looking at old barns and talking to retired barn framers. "A barn is like a living thing," she had told me. "Each different kind of grain has its mow, and each animal has its pen or stall, with its own manger. And every barn has its manure yard." I could smell the manure, of course, and I knew that it too had its purpose, since farming in the Pennsylvania-German way used it as fertilizer.

Thinking about all this, I walked up the ramp to the large doors that opened onto the threshing floor. As I stepped onto the wide surface, I realized I could hear male voices.

"Let us see! Come on; let us look!"

The two brothers stood together, their backs to me. As I walked toward them, I could see between their shoulders to where the tramp boy stood, facing them a little way beyond.

He didn't look afraid, exactly, but he looked wary. I crept closer, and I saw that he had his feet set apart, to keep his balance, and he held something close to his body, protected by both hands.

"Now we know where you go, when we can't find you," David, the older brother, said.

Without being able to help it, the tramp boy's dark eyes glanced upward, to a mow filled with gleaming hay.

"Show us what you do when you're by yourself," commanded the younger brother, Samuel, in a tone as much like David's as he could make it.

"I'll show you, but not now," said the tramp boy, holding his ground. "Not until it's ready."

Samuel began to clap his hands, teasingly. "Show us now! Show us now!"

"Not yet. You won't know what it is."

"Try us! Try us!" the two brothers chanted, and they began to press closer and closer to him.

"Your mother wants him!" I called out, unable to stand any more. They had made me angry, pushing toward him like that. "Let him be, so he can go in."

Maybe I had startled them; they stepped apart, looking sheepish and embarrassed. They changed from a pair of taunting bullies to two mild brothers, stepping back and turning to face me.

"He can go," David said. "We only wanted to know what he does here in his spare time."

The tramp boy, still holding whatever he had hidden against his body, didn't speak. I saw his eyes on me, dark with emotion; a patch of red still gleamed in each cheek.

No longer held captive by their teasing, he walked steadily toward me. He wore a leather carpenter's apron, as I now could see, and as we walked out of the barn and down its ramp, he pushed what he had been holding into the apron's side pocket.

"Is that your apron?" I asked, for something cheerful to say.

"Yes. I brought it with me when I came here."

"Oh." I remembered the rolled up form that he had held in his arms when I first saw him. "You're needed to help with the flax."

"Good," he said.

As we went around to the side porch, where on mild days we could still sit in the shade and look out across the creek as it flowed past the house, leaves dotted the water's dappled surface, and young evergreens, which had begun to grow again along its banks since the days when this part of the farm had been cleared, reached out dark green arms.

"Do you know how to break and scutch flax?" I asked.

"If I don't," he replied, "I can learn."

"There you are, just in time," Barbara said, approvingly, looking up as we came onto the porch. "Here, you can do this," she told the tramp boy.

She pointed to the flax break. Shaped like a long box, it formed a long horizontal slot. Above it, there was a slab of flat wood that could be raised and lowered from its hinged end by a handle. The shabby grey flax, no longer standing green and proud with its blue flowers dotted over its field, had been dew-retted, laid on the grass under every weather, until it looked spoiled and old and good for nothing. But inside its husk, it had a second life.

"Lay the flax on the break like this," she told him. She picked up a swatch, arranged its stems all in the same direction, and then, grasping it firmly, she laid it across the waiting slot. With a series of firm strokes, she brought the hinged slab down on the flax swatch, again and again. The rough, dried covering broke away, and as she worked, the swatch grew more and more supple.

"I can do that," the tramp boy said, and he took up a swatch for himself and went to work, breaking it.

"Now you," Barbara told me, and led me to the scutcher.

"I know how to do it," I said, looking at the short wooden post, attached to its wooden base. The job, though back-breaking because you had to bend over, was extremely simple. Choosing a bundle of broken flax about as big as a man's thumb, and as long as a horse's tail, I grasped it in my left hand and laid it with its thicker end on the flat top of the post which formed the upright section of the scutcher. Then, taking a longish, wooden scutching knife in my right hand, I began to press the loosened fibres of the upper stalk, moving the knife downward, so that the strands of flax hung like thick hair, showering its broken covering of straw onto the flat board below.

I went on doing this until the fine fibres hung loosely, shining like the locks of a girl's fair hair. The tramp boy and I both bent over these simple wooden machines, breaking and scutching the flax. We were too busy to speak, but as we worked, our movements gradually began to come into rhythm with each other.

Leaving us to our tasks, Barbara turned to the last stage of the process, hackling. The hackle looked downright dangerous, I thought. It combined a flat wooden slab with big, sharp spikes of black iron, pointing up like a bed of nails. Barbara, looking peaceful and mild, pulled the swatches that we thought we had already stripped clean, again and again between the iron teeth. When she finished, the flax fell softly into a fine cascade, gleaming and luminous. She smiled a little, just to herself, with pleasure at its beauty.

Through our work, all those faded and broken strands of dirty straw now shone and gleamed like gold.

"Look," I said to the tramp boy, pointing to the finished flax strands. "Good as new!"

He didn't stop what he was doing, but he sighed, almost too softly to be heard, but not quite. "Everything has to die before it can be made new," he answered.

When Louisa and Lydia came home from school with Mary, who had been sent to get them, they had something to do, too. In the process of breaking the flax, its seeds, hidden in tiny globe-shaped pods, had fallen, along with their little stems, onto a cloth, set out to catch them. Mary, ready to take her part, brought out a huge and heavy brass mortise and pestle, a bell-shaped, cuplike vessel set on a flat base, with a fat grinder, round and large at one end and narrower at the other, inside.

"There," she said, with a gasp.

The young girls took turns with the two parts of their job. Lydia carefully rubbed handfuls of seed pods between her palms until their pale coverings broke up, letting out the tiny black seeds inside, and she blew away the husks, leaving the shiny seeds in her cupped hand. Louisa poured a handful of these husked seeds into the bottom of the mortar, and ground them around and around inside with the fat end of the pestle, until each one had given up its oil.

I remembered being told that flax seed oil could be used for all sorts of things, from oiling and polishing, to some kinds of old-fashioned medicines.

We spent the whole of an unexpectedly mild day at these tasks, except the part we spent on dinner, all working together in silence, accompanied by the soft sounds of flax, being broken without complaint, and of the seeds being ground as the mortar rang with a low-pitched note while the pestle turned around inside it, and the occasional giggles of the younger girls.

Our work held us all as if we were under a spell, almost as if our hearts had begun to beat in unison, or we somehow all breathed in and out together at the same time. The mild wind smelled of fallen leaves and evergreen boughs; I could hear, even at that distance, the sound of the pigeons in the roofs of the buildings behind the house.

Finally, the mother called to us from the side door, "You'd best be finishing up, or the others will be in for supper before we've put it on the table."

That didn't mean we put down our work and left it right away. She had warned us in time to let us stop, lay the gathered swatches of shining flax in bundles of exactly the right size and shape for spinning, sweep up the scattered fragments of fibre that would have uses of its own, and clean and put away all the implements we had used so they would be ready when we next needed their help.

As we were finishing all this, the tramp boy stopped beside me with a basket of sweepings in his arms. "I'm glad you came to the barn when you did," he said, in a low voice.

I looked at him. "I'm glad too."

"Do you want to see what I was making?"

"Only if you want me to," I answered, but of course I did want to see it.

"I'd rather wait until it's finished, but I will show it to you, just because you didn't ask." With a quick motion he set aside his basket, and slipped his hand into one of the deep pockets of his leather apron.

When he pulled it out, I saw the beginnings of a carven figure, a small, graceful shape cut from some sweet-smelling, richly coloured wood. The shape looked teasingly familiar, but I couldn't be sure what it was. And I feared to ask, as if my question might somehow spoil this lovely and unexpected chance.

"Don't you want to know what it is?" he whispered.

"If I'm allowed."

He held out his scarred palm, and I put the unfinished carving there, its shape as delicate and indistinct as a cloud, and its wood as fragrant as morning.

"Of course you are allowed," he said. "But I don't know for sure what it is myself, yet. It all depends on the grain of the wood. I have an idea, but the wood has ideas too. I promise you, though, you'll know what it is when I know what it is. So you can be sure that you'll find out when the time comes."

And then, before I could say another word, he slipped the carving back into the apron's pocket, hefted his basket, and walked away.

The sisters had moved along the porch and into the kitchen, and the tramp boy followed them. I stood alone, in silence, breathing the last sweet air of a day I had never expected, and which I assumed would never come again. As I moved along the porch toward the door with its heart-shaped, wrought iron latch, I felt the first breath of a cool wind, coming no longer from the south but from the north, a wind that promised a cold night and a changed morning.

Chapter Five: The Bushlot

Most of my time now went to clearing the last of the good things still left in the garden, in company with the other girls, and then carefully rebuilding the four square-shaped planting beds, so that they rose up like islands defined by the two crossed paths dividing them. We smoothed out the paths as well, and bundled up the bean poles to take indoors so they wouldn't split in the coming cold, and dug out the winter vegetables to store in the cellar. We piled straw on top of the empty beds to protect them through the winter.

We raked the yard, too, pulling away the leaves as they fell like golden flocks of migratory birds, and banking them up so they could cover whatever needed shelter, or burning them down along the roadside near the creek crossing, a job that filled the air with the sweetest-smelling smoke that ever was.

The garden, the lawn, and the orchard were women's work, though the boys did help with the raking. The men of the house had their own work, and every time they came back to the side porch, they left mud and a smell of manure to show the kind of work they did.

Indoors, as well as outdoors, plenty of work kept the girls busy too. Everything grown out-of-doors either had to be stored raw, or cooked and then stored. That meant baskets and baskets of apples, already put down cellar, fragrant as wine, and still more apples cut and put to boil for apple butter, stirred for hours over a slow fire on a space of bare earth worn flat in the yard, until it grew dark and thick, and then was ladled into earthenware jugs and covered with paper and string. The boys, when they had time, took turns stirring the apple butter in the big black kettle, but the rest of the time that job was ours.

Everything had a particular way of being preserved and stored, and the mother and her daughters and I all worked together, talking sometimes, and other times, singing. Many of their songs were hymns, which they all knew by heart.

Most of these came from the *Lieder-Sammlung*, a songbook they used when they went to church at their meeting house.

Of the books I saw in that house—Bishop Benjamin Eby's *ABC*, a book of lessons for children which had been printed in Waterloo

County, the Bible in Martin Luther's translation, a version of Foxe's *Book of Martyrs*, which had terrifying pictures in it that gave me nightmares for days afterwards, and a prayer book called the *Paradiesgärtlein*, the Paradise Garden, whose pictures were as beautiful and reassuring as any I'd ever seen—the *Lieder-Sammlung* was certainly not used least. The words of some of its songs yearned for home, written by a people in exile, whether from their homelands in Europe, or from paradise, lost and longed for. Others sang of a place, in the woods or on the mountainsides, where one could live at peace in a little hut, where every day would be a Sabbath rest from work or sorrow. One song, however, I had not yet heard sung; it came later, and I never forgot it afterwards.

During all this time, I saw little of the tramp boy. He and the father and the brothers spent all their days in the fields, busy with the work of clearing what could be cleared, and ploughing under whatever was left, preparing the earth for its winter rest. Some parts, I knew, would get an even longer rest, being given their turn to lie fallow, not to be used for a year or more, and then returned to service while another field had a chance to recover its strength. This, along with changing the crops assigned to each field in a regular rotation, allowed the earth to be renewed, so that these wise farmers never had to see their fields become weak and worn out.

The big barn not only kept their animals safe, but also meant the farmers didn't have to kill them back to only a seed herd every year. And, as the many creatures sheltered in their stalls and stables, they also stood outside in the manure yard, where their numbers kept them from becoming too cold, and they produced mountains of manure, not to be wasted, but to be dug back into the fields to enrich the earth even more. I didn't envy the boys that job, back-breaking and so strong smelling that their mother sometimes made them change their clothes before they came into the house.

Finally, one morning, early enough to show a mist lying over the fields and make ghosts of the trees that now looked skinny and forlorn with half their leaves fallen, as I came out of the privy, I heard a soft voice speaking my name.

"Oh!" I gasped. "You scared me."

The tramp boy stood in the lane that led between the out-buildings and the barn, dressed for the morning chill. I had draped a heavy shawl over my shoulders and wore thick stockings in my dew-dampened shoes, but still, I shivered.

He said nothing more, but put a finger to his lips, signalling me to be silent.

Then he turned, beckoning but still unspeaking, and led me away into the mist, beyond the last outbuilding, as the lane gave way to a narrow path that went toward the bushlot covering the western parts of the farm. The family owned many acres—nearly four hundred—and not all of it had been cleared. Our path led upstream along the creek, and in the strange foggy silence I could hear the sound of running water, as the creek, not yet frozen, made its soft music between the grassy banks.

As we went, the fog began to lift, or maybe the trees became easier to see as we approached them. The tramp boy walked along steadily ahead, not looking to the right or the left, until we reached a long, low building with a slanted roof held up by stout posts instead of walls. I had been there once before, sent to bring an earthenware jug of water to the thirsty workers, so I knew this place as a sawmill. It had been built and was still operated by the family; the creek's dam stood above the point where the sawmill was located, and the pressure of the water turned a big wooden wheel that drove the sawblade, spilling sweet sawdust. Water poured over the top of the wheel, making it move majestically for-ward and down and then back and under, singing and creaking.

But this morning the wheel stood still; the water had been allowed to flow past. The sawmill and its sharp-toothed circular saw blade rested and waited, while the water flowed fast, with a sound like chuckling laughter, as if it were glad to be free. Stacks of bright, clean, freshly cut lumber stood neatly piled beside the silent blade, smelling so fragrant that it made me want to cry, made me think of Christmas trees now lost and far away. The life of the trees still lived in that sap-filled wood, and the lumber need-ed to cured, to be dried over time, so that it could be used with-out splitting and cracking, and spoiling its carpenters' work.

43

"Come," the tramp boy whispered, beckoning me to follow him further. We walked on past the sawmill, moving closer and closer to the bushlot, where many tall white pines still rose up, their complex branches bearing bursts of long, deep green, curved needles, and their roots spread out in the earth. Between them the ground had been covered with a carpet of brown pine needles; little underbrush barred our way in this forest, and we could have moved easily among those trees.

But that wasn't what we did.

Instead, the tramp boy stopped, and gestured to me to stop too. We stood there in silence, so long that I began to be cold and numb, shivering where I stood. I pulled my shawl tightly around myself, and still we stood on, not speaking.

Then, without warning, almost without a sound, a tall stag came toward us, emerging from the green darkness at the heart of the bushland, slipping easily and lightly between the rough, grey tree trunks. I could see the creature's beautiful warm, brown coat and lighter underbody, his upheld head with his black nose, his bright amber eyes, and, rising from above his brow, the pair of outspread antlers.

I forgot to breathe. I held as still as I could, though I trembled where I stood. The stag moved toward us, without, as far as I could see, the slightest fear.

Ever so gently he approached, until, quite beyond reason, he placed his delicate, velvety muzzle into the outstretched, open, upturned palm of the tramp boy. The wonderful eyes, like glistening chestnuts, rolled up to gaze into his face, and the boy placed his other hand upon the broad, horned brow as a mother or father might have touched a favourite child.

They looked at each other for a long, long time, or so it seemed to me. Then, the tramp boy took away one hand, dug it deep in his coat pocket, and pulled out a small green apple, dappled with specks, the longest-lasting apple of the year, last to be put down and sweet to the very end. This he presented on his open hand, and the stag took it delicately from him, nodding the crest of his horns as if in thanks. Several more small apples followed the first, and, his offering complete, the boy stroked the stag's soft nose for a moment, then, gently, moved away backwards, showing me with the flat of his hand swept back that I, too, ought to retreat, and leave the majestic beast to his privacy and peace.

The stag turned suddenly, sprang away into the dusk of the woods, and was gone. We walked back more slowly than we had come, as if this contact with the earth had tired us, taking away some part of our power.

"How did you make him come to you?" I whispered, when we were nearly halfway back to the farmstead.

"I didn't make him. He came of his own accord."

"Has he come before?"

"Oh, yes. Often. It's best to visit him very early; I got up before the others."

"Really!" Farmboys went to work well before light, all year long. In the late fall, that could be very early indeed.

"He comes because I feed him. It isn't magic."

I laughed. "I guess not. But it seemed to be."

Then we walked on together until we reached the rearmost building of the farmstead. Without another word, he separated himself from me, heading around the back of the smokehouse, toward the barn.

Sighing, I walked on alone. When I stepped up onto the side porch, the kitchen door opened suddenly, startling me so that I stopped where I stood.

"There you are," the mother greeted me with a hoarse whisper, whisking her shawl around her shoulders as she came. "Have you seen our tramp boy?"

"Yes." My heart gave a thump as I realized that two teenagers alone in the woods might mean something else to her than feeding wild deer.

"When? Where?"

"Just now," I answered, speaking as quietly as I could. "When I was at the privy. I think he went toward the barn."

I held my crossed fingers behind my back—it wasn't a lie, I told myself, but it wasn't quite all of the truth, either. Then, seeing a look of real distress on her face, I added, "Why? What's the matter?"

She didn't answer right away. She looked into my eyes as if she was looking for something there; the truth, I suppose.

Then, she spoke. "A man has come, looking for his runaway apprentice. At least, that's what he says."

I had been anxious before. This made me truly afraid. "Is it true, then?"

"I don't know. It may be. Father's out in the fields with our sons, but I didn't see which way they went."

"Is the man still here?"

This time she paused even longer before answering. Finally, "No," she said, "I told him we had no tramp boy with us. At least, I told him there' d been a boy, but he'd gone."

At that, I threw my arms around her, and she wrapped hers around me, and we hugged as if we were a mother and daughter meeting after a long separation. Nothing more needed to be said. We had agreed without speaking. I knew she had understood, that she knew just as I did that the tramp boy could never safely be given up to his harsh master.

"Maybe he hid in the barn," I said, as we stood apart, looking at each other as if we were meeting, really meeting, for the first time.

"I expect so. But I'm sure the man will come back."

I shook my head. "I wish he wouldn't."

"I wish so too. But he'll want to reclaim his property. That's the way he'll see it. He wasn't a generous man."

Then she smiled, a gentle smile, and looked down at my shoes, muddy, of course, from my long, early walk to the bushlot. "Feeding the deer, were you?" she asked.

"Yes. How did you know?"

"I followed him once, and saw what he did."

After that, I felt safe to ask my last question, speaking very carefully. "Did you tell—did you tell the father—what you had seen?"

"Of course. I tell him everything."

"Of course," I echoed, and we went into the kitchen together.

Chapter Six: Sausage Making

After that, everybody in the house behaved differently. The parents solemnly called us all together in the sitting room, where we sat up straight and listened in silence, feeling very odd to be there on a weekday.

"You're not to go into town without permission, and even then, you mustn't go alone," Sarah told us, while Joseph nodded in agreement. Clearly, they had talked the matter over together.

The boys looked annoyed; I knew they liked to slip away sometimes, just to see the sights. Not often, but enough to satisfy their curiosity about the new buildings beginning to go up, and the new shops opening. They didn't say anything out loud, of course.

"And even then, nobody can go without our Barbara," Sarah continued, as if she knew what her sons had been thinking. "And you're not to take her away from her work too often; she's busy enough as it is, and she has the making of her trousseau on top of that."

"What about taking the little ones to school?" I asked, and everybody turned to look at me.

"You are right," she said to me, nodding and smiling. "I've seen you looking at our books. Do you think you could teach the little girls their letters?"

"Why can't we go to school?" Lydia asked.

"It's just for a little while, just till we're sure that everything's all right."

"Oh."

"So," Sarah continued, "could you teach them, just for a few days?"

I didn't know whether I could or not, but I answered, "I can try."

She nodded her head. "Good."

David, the oldest boy, held up his hand. "I can take turns walking the others to town, so nobody has to be the one to go all the time."

Joseph smiled. "Good idea," he said, and David blushed and held himself up proudly.

After this family meeting, David and Barbara became even more solemn and dignified than they had already been. I could understand that; I was an eldest child too.

The next day I led Louisa and Lydia upstairs to the spare bedroom at the back of the house, where Sarah set out a table and three chairs so I could teach them their lessons. I tried to remember what I had been taught at their age, but I realized that a lot of it would have been impossible for them to understand. What would they make of television, and computers, and automobiles, and airplanes?

After thinking about it, I decided to let them show me what they had already learned, so I could go on from there.

"Can we show you?" Louisa asked.

"Of course. A good teacher is always ready to learn." I had heard Mama say that.

"All right," Louisa agreed, and climbed up onto her chair, while her younger sister, Lydia, pressed close against her to watch.

I had taken out the *ABC*, and looked through its pages.

"Have you read this?" I asked.

"Part of it," Louisa answered.

"I can name the letters," Lydia added.

"Right. Good. Let's begin."

Slowly, and with some hesitation, Louisa opened the book, and turned its pages, looking at the illustrations. "Here's something I like," she said.

She put her finger on the page, where a picture showed a schoolmaster, dressed in a long black costume, sitting in front of a tall desk with a large book open upon it. Three children stood behind a desk, watching, and two sat on little benches, leaning over a low table, reading. But the teacher in the picture was not watching them. He looked down mildly at a child who stood directly in front of him, holding out an open book.

Both of my little students pored over the picture, and Louisa ran her finger under the lines of German, printed in Gothic lettering.

"It's a poem," she said. Obviously, this old printing style didn't discourage her; I decided to give it a try too, and found myself reading it aloud:

> *Dear children, look and see*
> *The school that's pictured there;*
> *The teacher teaching thee,*
> *As he sits upon his chair.*

"I wanted to read it!" my older pupil complained.

"Oh. All right. You read the second verse."

> *See how the children busily*
> *Read, count and write their rhymes;*
> *How virtuously and piously*
> *They spend their noble times.*

"What's 'piously'?" she asked; she had sounded out the word without understanding it.

"It means a person who likes to pray, or something like that," I answered.

"This is not a prayer book."

"No. But there's one here, if you want to read it."

"No. Thank you. I am reading this one," she said. She put her finger to the first line of the third verse.

> *Follow these good children here,*
> *And learn with equal vigour;*
> *Thus may you be, each year,*
> *More pious, better, wiser.*

"Pious again," she said. "There, I've read it."

"Very good! You're a clever one, I can see that."

"Pious? Better? Wiser?" She had begun to giggle.

"Wise enough for now, anyway."

"Can I read?" Lydia asked.

"Yes. Here, change places, the two of you."

Louisa moved over and I sat down with Lydia on my lap.

"You tell me the words, and I'll say them," she said.

"Good idea. Now, here we go."

I read each line out loud, and she repeated it. While we did this, Louisa took the prayer book from our pile of books, just as I had suggested, and began to turn the pages. I could hear her whispering words, though the book must have been beyond her level.

Each day we read something, and did simple arithmetic, and I told stories, and they drew pictures on their slates with their slate pencils. I had begun to feel, more than before, like a part of their family.

I didn't know exactly what the tramp boy thought about all these precautions, but I felt sure he had noticed them. His face became distant and closed; if he had once looked boyish, he lost all trace of that now. I kept hoping for a flash of the sweetness I had seen in him, but all I could find was a careful watchfulness, and sometimes, far worse, a look of grim expectation, as if he knew from hard experience what would, sooner or later, come to him again.

Nobody could enter a room with him in it, without his level gaze being shot exactly at them, followed, sometimes, by a soft sigh, not of relief, but of briefly relaxed attention. More and more, he looked like a lantern whose light had burned down so low that it would take no more than a breath to blow it out.

Once, when I found him alone in the kitchen, I spoke to him. "Are you still working on your carving?"

After his quick look at me as I came in, he lowered his eyes. "Sometimes," he answered.

"Do you know yet what it is going to be?"

"Not yet."

"Will you show it to me, really, when it is finished?"

That brought his eyes back to me. "I promised I would, and if I can finish it, and if I can show it to you, I will," he said. "But I can't be sure now what will happen."

I had no answer to that; I couldn't be sure what would happen either. We stood together for a moment, in silence; then we both heard a step on the porch outside, and he walked away.

In spite of the tension everybody felt, made worse by the fact that nobody in the family talked about it, we had little time to brood. November would be coming soon, as we all knew, with its stiff frosts and bone-chilling winds. And the last of October promised to bring some new excitement.

"We'll be having a butchering soon," Sarah said to Barbara, one cold bright morning when we had lingered over a cup of tea. "But first we've promised to help the Martins with theirs."

"Can we go this year?" Barbara asked.

I understood that the family would certainly have gone as always, if it hadn't been for the tramp boy and the danger that threatened him.

"Your father will go, of course," her mother told her. "And your brothers."

"You should go too," Barbara said. "I'll stay home."

"Thank you, but I have to be here this year. You and the other big girls should be there, because the women from both families will be needed." Then, unexpectedly, Sarah turned to me. "You can go along with our girls; they'll show you what to do."

I'm sure I showed by my face how happy this made me; Sarah smiled, and pushed her cup away.

Just as she stood up from the table, the tramp boy came in with an armful of kindling. "Stop a minute," she told him.

He put the kindling down beside the stove, and then stood still, his face alert as it always was when she spoke to him.

"A butchering is set for next week," she said.

I couldn't tell what he thought of that. He only waited, silent.

"But I'm staying home this year," she continued. "And somebody has to stay home and help with the chores."

He nodded, and I caught a brief glimpse of the mild face I had seen often before, and now saw rarely.

So I went to the butchering, and what I saw there I never forgot. It proved to be a day without wind, clear and cool. When we arrived after the long ride on the road that led out among other Mennonite farms, we found the fire already burning, its smoke rising straight up into the blue air. Set above it, the great blackened vessel of water was already hot, and the butcher was hard at work.

Freshly killed by a blow from a heavy wooden mallet, a hog rose up, pulled by ropes slung over pulleys that lifted it free of the ground. I stood still and watched; I couldn't take my eyes away. As fast as lightning, the butcher drove in his long, well-sharpened knife, and pulled downwards with all his strength, to open the animal's body and let out a spill of intestines and other organs which the women caught, falling, to make sure these important parts landed where they should, in a large trough below. The women separated the intestines from the other organs, all of them good to eat, whether stomach or liver or heart.

What could they want with the intestines, that great mass of slithering tubes? With six pigs to be slaughtered in all, there would be tubsful to deal with.

During the rest of the day, the carcasses were taken apart, the butcher carefully separating them just as if he were a carpenter cutting up wood, to be made into bacon, and ribs, and hams, tenderloins, shoulders, headcheese, and even tails and feet. The fat, too, found a place, to be cut up and boiled until all the oil came out, and rendered down into lard when it was cooked and cooled. Every last scrap had a use; the women packed it into baskets to use for making sausage.

A few days later, the Martins came in their turn to help us with our butchering, and after they left, our sausage making began.

First we all sat outside in the cool air, cleaning the gobbets of fat from the long tubes of the intestines. Then we washed these tubes, which flopped and curved around themselves like old wet nylon stockings, to get them perfectly clean, turning them inside out after we cut them into manageable length, to be sure they were perfect. Last, the mother blew through each carefully measured section, to check that it had no holes, except at each end.

Next we helped to mince the big basketfulls of meat scraps as finely as we could, and put all we had prepared into a tub. We seasoned it with lovage and thyme and pepper and salt, along with maple sugar. We boiled this, and it smelled wonderful, so that we wished we could eat it right away.

Almost nothing happens right away on a farm, as I had found out already, and the filling we had made still had to be forced into the lengths of intestine to make sausages. We used a big iron sausage stuffer to do this.

The tramp boy, who had been advised to stay in his room while our visitors helped us with the butchering, was now pressed into service, the Martin family having gone home with many goodbyes and thank yous. He sat down as he was told, holding the upper end of each prepared length of intestine, while I, standing up, pressed the meat we had chopped and seasoned into the top of the sausage stuffer. Between us, David lifted a long-handled lever up, and pushed it down, to force the sausage into each tube of intestine until it had been filled. Barbara and Mary tied the ends of each tube with string, and twisted portions of it around to divide the whole tube into a series of lengths.

By the time we finished, we had many strings of beautiful pale pink sausage, looking like gleaming marble and ready to be parboiled. Sarah, with Louisa and Lydia, stood at the stove, making sure the big cooking pots didn't boil over.

Most of the sausages we made together were put into crocks and sealed in lard, and set down in the cool cellar to keep, at least for a while. But some of the sausages we cooked right away. Sarah popped them into a big black frying pan, and fried them on the stove, making the whole house smell so delicious that we could hardly bear it.

"Something smells good," the father said, stamping in from outside.

"We won't go hungry this year," his wife told him, and they smiled at each other.

"Praise God for that," he replied.

We ate the fried sausages for supper, hot and fragrant and fresher than any sausages I had ever tasted. We took big chunks of bread—the other children did this first, and I did it too, after watching them—and wiped them across the plates to get up every last tasty drop of hot grease and every bit of sausage. The mother went back to the stove and fried more slices of bread in the grease that had been left in the frying pan, so that nothing at all would be wasted. Then we ate applesauce and dried apple pie to fill up any of the empty spaces.

Other kinds of sausage that didn't need to be fried had to be made, too; these had been stuffed into cloth tubes and would be smoked in the smokehouse. Sausages cured by smoking would keep for ages; they hung in ropes from pegs set into the wall to keep them safe from mice. Other cuts of meat had to be salted and smoked too, or preserved in other ways, some by oiling and setting aside in gelatine with paper covers tied in string. Loveliest of all to eat were the big hams, aged in brine and smoked for a long, long time, and then wrapped in cloths and kept to be served for the very best occasions, when company would come. The hams would be sliced thinly by the mother with her sharpest knife, after she had boiled them to make them tender, and served on great platters to the hungry guests.

"Do you think the hogs know how useful they are?" I asked her.

"I can't say," she answered. "But after we've helped them to farrow, and fed them slops from our own table, and tickled them around their ears when they've come to the fence on their little feet, and left them to lounge all day on the manure pile, keeping warm, I should think they would understand that it was a fair exchange."

I thought about that. Then, "And do they know what's going to happen to them?"

"Of course not! How could they know?"

"I just wondered." I began to be sorry I had asked.

Maybe she heard in the tone of my voice what I had begun to feel. "There's a difference between you and any little piglet, no matter how dear and pink it looks," she said.

"We're people and they're pigs?"

"No," she answered. Then, in a more serious voice than before, she explained. "Human folk know they must die someday. Hogs don't."

After that, I said nothing more.

Chapter Seven: The Lamb's Table

"Come down quick! Company's here!" Samuel cried, dashing in from the veranda where he had been snatching a moment of early November sunlight after several days of rain.

Sure enough, his sharp eyes had spied, far away south along the muddy road that led away into the farmlands, a buggy coming along smartly. As it moved closer, several of us joined him there, staring and trying to guess whose buggy we saw. Samuel named the family before the rest of our watchers could decide; I knew he'd be right. He could identify every horse he had seen by its gait long before anyone else. And he'd know everything else about it too; how many hands tall it stood, its age, and its colouring, long before the driver or passengers could be recognized.

When the buggy finally arrived, coming along the lane to the side porch, we all welcomed our visitors, whose daughter was best friends with our Barbara.

"We've set the day for the wedding!" the young woman said, after her mother, having reined in the great-hipped horse, had alighted. Samuel took charge of the horse, with a glance for permission from its driver. He loosed its reins and led it around toward the barn, where he should have been anyway, at that hour of the day. He would stand for hours, if allowed, feeding a horse handfuls of oats, and whispering into its ears.

We all began to talk at once, Sarah included, as she came to the side porch, drying her hands on her apron. She had shown the motherly good sense to throw on her shawl, while the rest of us stood shivering in the cold morning.

"Hush, now, you sound like a flock of geese," she joked, and she and her visitor went into the kitchen, where I felt sure they would have a long and satisfying visit. The rest of us pulled our visitor's daughter toward the stairway, heading for our bedroom where we could have a talk.

"Don't stay too long; we've a lot to get ready for when Father and the boys come in for dinner," Sarah said, and I heard her invite her guest to stay for the meal.

Then, in joyous privacy, we all heard and shared in the news of the coming wedding. Barbara listened in silence, thinking, I supposed, of her own wedding, yet to come. After we had heard, and exclaimed about, the whole report, our guest put out both her hands and clasped the hand of our Barbara.

"Now for my question," she said.

"Question?" little Lydia asked, and all the girls laughed at once, not harshly or to make fun, but sweetly, like bells, in the joy of what they knew would come next.

"Would you," the young woman asked, her dark eyes bright and her cheeks pink with excitement, "would you be part of our bridal party? You and your intended, to be one of the six couples?"

I saw Barbara smile, her hands clasped in her effort at self control. "I will," she said, "with all my heart."

I knew, because I had heard Sarah say so, that not every family could give a wedding as complex as the one our visitor's family would have, and I knew that Barbara knew it too. I wondered if I would have been able to hide my feelings as well as she did, that morning. Being an eldest sister had its advantages, but it had its responsibilities, too.

From the day of this visit to the day of the wedding, besides the regular chores of our household, we made and stored the good things we would bring to help our family's friends and fellow church members prepare for the wedding feast. Among the many pies and cakes and cookies we baked and wrapped and set aside in the pie safe, the one I wanted most to taste was the wedding bread.

Flavoured with saffron to make it golden and fragrant at the same time, and anise—the seed that tasted like licorice—and honey, and cloves, the wedding bread smelled, I thought, like the pastures of heaven. The great round fat loaves of this wonderful bread stood stacked in a hempen sack, making everybody who came into the kitchen dizzy with anticipation.

The day we baked it, the tramp boy came to the side porch, and stood on the threshold. I could see that he smelled the wedding bread; he sniffed the air like a wild thing from the forest, scenting what? Danger? Loss? Somebody needed but far away?

His eyes, as I watched him, filled with tears. He put up his work-stained fingers and brushed them away from his red, chapped cheeks. Then his eyes swept the room, meeting mine, and in a flash he shook off whatever memory had hurt him, and gave me an unexpected smile, like sudden sunshine on a winter day. I smiled back, but the look of him hit me in the heart with a terrible nostalgia for my own world, far away, and sometimes even half forgotten.

When the wedding day arrived, the real sun shone through a haze of fine ice crystals, giving a strange light, dull and glaring at the same time.

"They've left this wedding very late in the year," our mother confided to her husband, and he nodded agreement.

Then he clucked at his horses, who responded together as they always did, their harness bells jingling as we went on our way to the wedding, each of us washed so clean that our hair squeaked, and our skin blazed pink and shiny from scrubbing and cold.

All of us went, that is, except for the tramp boy.

"You'll watch the house for us, will you?" Sarah asked him, and he agreed. "Stay close, now; the animals shouldn't be left alone so near to town. Everything's getting too big; more folk and fewer good ones, so it seems."

As we sat in the carriage, I saw him, standing alone behind the wavering glass of a window; his face looked pale and his eyes were shadowed. Sarah had promised to bring him some of the treats, but he knew—we all knew—why he could not come.

He would stay hidden, surely, I told myself; who would know he had been left behind? But as we drove away toward the south, I looked back, no longer able to see him, as the barn and the house disappeared behind a hill.

"You'll turn into salt, like Lot's wife!" Barbara teased.

"Maybe you'll marry a tramp boy one of these days," Mary added.

"Hush," their mother told them, not crossly, but firmly, "and remember you're not to mention him at the wedding. He's his own business, not yours, and he's our guest, so we are bound to keep him safe."

After that, they all fell silent.

The long, cold ride, that left our cheeks so bright that they looked painted, came at last to an end as we drove into a lengthy lane and stopped close by the tall house of a large farmstead, twice the size of ours. Each of us had something to carry inside, entering by the kitchen door.

Hugs, laughter, and the welcome warmth of a heavily laden stove all greeted us. We put our offerings where we could find room, and the daughter of the family led us by the hand to see her wedding table and the row of twelve chairs, where our big sister and her intended, along with the other specially chosen couples, would sit as witnesses from the community.

All the furnishings of the sitting room had been moved aside to make space for two large, long tables, where the wedding guests would be served. In a side room, opening from the sitting room, a smaller but more elaborately set table had been prepared for the wedding party, I saw the four stout legs that supported a handsome table, which had deep drawers opening on one side.

On top lay places for the bride, the groom, and the six couples, set with brightly painted china plates and cups and saucers, that must have been imported from far away. The bishop would sit at another table, along with the parents of the bride and groom, and the oldest uncles and aunts, set where they could see the newlyweds celebrating. I knew all this because the sisters had talked of nothing else but the wedding since the bride and her mother had paid us their visit.

China dishes, I thought. Not everybody in the community practised holy poverty, I could see that. "Holy poverty," I said aloud, in a whisper. Those were two of Daddy's favourite words; he used to quote them to me when he read one of his many books, the ones about the "desert fathers." The thought of him, coming suddenly as I stood beside that table, brought small tears, which I brushed away before anybody could see them.

Later on, when everything had been made ready, we gathered, the many families crowded together, to see the bridal party come in. The bride's friend—our Barbara—entered, with her golden hair peeping from under her cap, and her intended, shaven until his face looked sore, with a very solemn expression in his eyes, followed by the rest of the young couples. All sat in the row of chairs that had been arranged for them, in front of the bishop, a small, dark-haired man with warm brown eyes and fine beard, whom I remembered handing out paper-wrapped sweets to the younger children in our family on a Sunday visit to our house some weeks before. Like all their bishops, he had been chosen by drawing lots, like St. Matthias, as I had thought when I first heard about this custom.

After a song from the *Lieder-Sammlung*, followed by a sermon, the young couple, their faces bright with excitement, stood up before the bishop and exchanged their vows of marriage in low, intense voices. The bride wore a handsome black wedding dress.

"You're going to wear black?" I had exclaimed, foolishly letting down my guard, when she had happily described this dress during her visit to us.

"Of course," she answered, "I'll be a wife, then, won't I?"

As part of his own finery, the groom wore a beautiful white wedding shirt, with the tiniest tucks in its cuffs, making a delicate ruffled pattern called "mouse teeth." Now, the bride and groom and the rest of the wedding party went to the side room to sit at their own table with its colourful china; the bishop sat at the head of the table, as the leader of the feast.

Then the songs began, the table songs sung especially for weddings and for funerals, when people sat at special tables while wonderful meals were served. This was the table song that I liked best:

> *Come at last to the Lamb's Table*
> *Here in Your Kingdom, let us eat*
> *The thousand gifts, fresh and gentle*
> *That You will measure out as meet.*
> *There we'll taste of Joy, of Honour,*
> *From Your hand, O Lord, and never*
> *Fail to sing Your praise forever.*

This song told about the Lamb's Table that would be set in Paradise, where everybody would sit down and feast forever. I began to understand why this bride wore black; she would die to her girlhood and her unmarried life, to become a new person, a wife, with all the enjoyment of marriage as well as all its responsibilities. Maybe, I thought, the black clothing worn at funerals, where this same song would be sung, showed that the dead, too, would begin new lives where everything would be joyful forever.

Listening to the table song, I imagined a garden full of beautiful flowers, where angels would bring in the heavenly food and drink, and the guests would look at each other with joy and surprise, each delighted to see the others and amazed to be there themselves, while the Person—I knew that the Lamb was really a Person—would take up a servant's towel and serve each one as an honoured guest.

"What are you dreaming about?" Sarah asked me, softly, waking me out of my reverie.

"Oh! I—the Lamb's Table," I stammered.

She smiled and put her hand over mine. "That's a good dream," she said.

A long time later, we all went home, sitting in the carriage very quietly because the excitement had tired us. The elder sister, in particular, looked very thoughtful. The air felt sharp and cold after the heat of the crowded house and the excitement of the company and the food.

I had tucked a piece of wedding bread into my linen pocket, where I hoped it wasn't breaking down into crumbs; I intended to give it to the tramp boy. As we swayed along through the frozen countryside of that late afternoon, over roads that had become hard as diamonds, I looked at the sinking sun, and saw, vivid and unexpected, a set of perfect sun dogs, two rainbow patterns, one on each side of the sun, like a pair of outriders, defining a circle nobody could see without them, keeping company with the sun's unbearable whiteness.

I knew that sun dogs were formed by ice crystals very high in the sky, reflecting the sunlight. But I never saw them as something as simple as that, and on this day, they looked dangerous, like a couple of crystal hunting dogs, the sun's companioning twins, travelling fast, on an errand of urgent and terrifying need.

When we came to our farmstead, Joseph Schneider drove along the lane and toward the drive shed set against the barn, where we jumped down, with our empty bags and platters, and walked around the back of the house and into the kitchen, while he stayed to see to his horses, young Samuel at his side. Those horses would get good care, I knew, after their long run in the cold, pulling a full carriage.

I went into the kitchen hoping to find it warm, but the fire had burned so low that the room felt chilly, almost frigid. When I hung up my shawl and bonnet on the wall beyond the stove, I shivered.

"Didn't you tell our tramp boy to keep the fire going?" Barbara asked her mother.

"I thought I did," she answered.

The younger girls peeped into the sitting room, and not finding anyone there, they tiptoed through the pantry and the storage room and their parents' bedroom, calling out. Lydia even ventured down the cellar steps, almost to the bottom, and came back quickly.

"Nobody's there!" she reported, big-eyed.

Louisa went upstairs and came down with the same news.

Then Joseph entered the kitchen.

"Did you see our tramp boy?" Sarah asked him.

"Why? Isn't he here?" His face grew grim, guessing the answer.

"Go upstairs and look again," Sarah told me, touching my arm. "Maybe the girls were too shy to look into his room. He might have fallen asleep, waiting for us."

I hurried up the stairs and pushed open the tramp-room door.

His bed, narrow and low, lay there neatly made up with its coverings tucked in tightly and the wool-stuffed comforter rolled as small as possible, like a fat sausage, at its foot. His few clothes hung tidily from a row of pegs on the side wall. Something, though, I did not see.

"He's not there," I reported, "but his clothes are, or at least most of them. Only one thing is gone."

"What?" Joseph asked.

"His carpenter's apron, the one with his woodworking tools in it."

"I'll just have another look in the barn," he said, and went out of the side door.

Without waiting to ask for permission, I followed him, and we went, with him in front and me behind, up the earthen ramp to the barn's big doors, and onto the threshing floor. We stood there in the centre of the tall space, and I could hear a rising wind whistling between the boards, which creaked and groaned as the air pressure dropped, and not for the better, I thought.

"Boy!" he called, in a sharp voice, half command and half anxiety. "Boy!"

High overhead, in one of the mows, a small sound answered. As we stared upward, a figure popped out from the tall heap of hay that had been stored in one of the topmost mows, fragrant and fresh when the sun had been hot and the fields as bright as a gold coin, and now piled high and dry, enough for a whole winter's use.

"Has he gone?" the tramp boy asked, in a low voice kept almost steady.

"Who?"

The tramp boy made no answer, but he came down the ladder as quickly as he could, moving stiffly, like a person who had crouched in silence without daring to move, for so long that all his limbs had turned to ice.

When he stood on the threshing floor in front of us, he looked up into the father's eyes, and stood straight, with his hands at his side, his strong fingers pressed against his leather apron.

"It was the man who calls himself my master," he said.

"He came in here?"

"While you were gone, he came to the house. I heard him, hammering on the veranda door, where strangers come. But he couldn't find me."

"I can see that," Joseph said, with a hint of a smile in his voice.

They stood facing each other without saying any more for at least a minute.

Then, "What does he want?" Joseph asked.

"He wants me."

"He wants his apprentice back, you mean."

"I am not his apprentice."

"Are you not? What's his claim on you, then?"

"He has no claim that would stand in the law."

"You are not his apprentice, truly?"

"Truly. I was apprenticed once, but not to him."

"Then, why...."

The tramp boy looked at me, with the face of a person who is afraid to talk about something in a child's company. I held myself as straight as I could, trying to look all of my nearly fourteen years. I could stand to hear it, whatever it was, I longed to tell him.

"I...," he began again, "I learned my trade from my uncle, my father's brother, and he taught me well and fairly. My mother's a widow, so my father couldn't pass on his own trade to me."

"What had your father been?"

I held my breath, waiting to find out.

"A carpenter," the tramp boy replied, proudly.

"Ah," Joseph breathed. He too had taken his father's trade when he took charge of the farm where we stood, as I knew.

"When he died, I apprenticed to my uncle, who is a cabinet-maker, and served my three years, as I was sworn to do. Then I came away with my new set of cabinetmaker's tools in my new carpenter's apron, and a suit of clothes...."

"Your freedom suit," Joseph said.

"Yes. All new and well made by my aunt. But they were my undoing."

"How?"

"I'd been free for no more than a day or so, when a man came along—I was on my way home—and offered me a ride, as a change from walking. He said he knew my mother—I told him I was going to her—and he said he would take me part of the way." Again, he looked at me.

"But he didn't do that?"

"No. He had one more errand to run, he told me, and needed to stop off there first."

"So he didn't take you home."

"No."

"Where did he take you, then?"

A look of pain, so sharp I could hardly bear to see it, filled the tramp boy's face. "He—I—he took me...," he stammered, helplessly.

Joseph turned to me. "They need you indoors, surely," he said, in a tone that expected no refusal, and away I had to go, without hearing what came next.

Chapter Eight: A Snowstorm

The following morning, the sky came down over the farmstead, almost as if the trees in the distant bushlot could reach it, if only they were a few branches higher. A grey, dim, gloomy darkness filled the house, forcing the frugal Sarah to light a candle in the kitchen; she set it on the table so that we could see to do our work as we sat there.

"We'll be making candles before you know it," she predicted, her hands occupied with sewing the hem of a little gown. "And I'll be surprised if the snow doesn't fly before nightfall."

"Teacher," Lydia said, tugging at my apron, "I can't see to read my book."

She had a tiny primer in her hand, even older than the *ABC*. Each page of it showed pictures illustrating the alphabet, with short verses saying something to help remember the particular letter. We had begun holding our classes in the kitchen as the days grew colder.

I pulled her onto my lap, so that she could place her book close to the candle. "What is this, then?" I asked, pointing to a picture.

"The Goose!"

"Very good. And that stands for G. Now, what is this?"

"The Hen!"

"And what letter does the Hen stand for?"

"An H," she told me.

"How does it sound?"

"Hhhh…," she breathed.

I gave her a hug. "What a good student you are!"

Louisa came to my chair and pressed against me. "I want to read too," she said, and I patted the empty chair at my side.

Up she hopped, and pointed to the next of the letters. "I know this. It's an 'I'," she said.

"Right. And what does the picture show?"

She pushed her nose down toward the page. "I'm not sure."

"Then I'll tell you. It's an island. Here's the word—I-S-L-A-N-D."

"What's an island?"

"Look, see how there's a little bit of land here, with trees and a house? And all around it, what do you see?" The picture showed a circle of waves, not like real waves, that I had seen when my family visited Lake Huron, but a row of wavy lines, like the scallops around a pie. I touched these imaginary waves. "The people on this island have to go across water to get anywhere else."

"Like crossing our creek to get to town?"

"Something like that."

Sarah chuckled, listening to this alphabet lesson. "Is our farm an island, then?" she asked.

I thought about this. "In a way it is," I agreed.

"When we go from the farm to the village, it is like going to a different world."

"Now you know why we live here instead of there," she said, and went back to her sewing.

After I and my pupils had talked about several more letters, and they had begun to squirm, I closed the book, and they scrambled down.

"There is something we need," I said to the mother, who sat quietly with her busy needle flashing in and out.

"What is that?"

"These children's lessons need to be written with a pen; it's hard to form their letters on a slate with a slate pencil."

"I'll be plucking the geese again soon," she said. "We'll have plenty of pens then, I promise you."

As I went to the cupboard to put away our school books and slates, I stopped at a window and looked out at the November world. The ground lay iron hard, with the grass flat and easily broken. The creek no longer gurgled by. No waves there, I thought, and smiled at what my pupils had said. Whatever flooding had filled that creek in the spring, had long since sunk deep into the earth or gone roaring away toward Lake Erie, far to the south where I had never visited in any century. Instead, a flat white sheet of ice, so thick it couldn't be broken, lay hard and cold on top of whatever water remained.

The boys had already tried this ice, early in the morning. I had seen them sliding over its surface in their heavy barn-soiled boots, shouting and slipping and falling until their father called them back and set them to some task or other. The tramp boy, who had showed himself more stable on the frozen surface than either of them, came away first, looking toward the house with bright cheeks and shining eyes, as if he had, at least for the moment, forgotten his fears and memories.

Then they all had gone off to the barn. Now, as I stood remembering this, I heard them coming back, and, as the mother set aside her sewing and stood up, we heard them stamping on the porch, as much to warm their feet as to shake off the frost. And in they came, clapping their hands to warm their stinging fingers, made colder by having to use them to ease off their boots, which they had set in a row at the door, padding across the cold wooden floor in their thick, knitted woollen stockings.

"Hang up your coats," the mother said, as she said every time they came into the house. In a moment I caught the smell of steamy wool as the coats were hung heavily on their pegs, near the stove.

The day went on, growing ever darker, as we cooked and sewed and scrubbed, and went about the business of our lives. Finally, late in the day, as I stood in front of the dry sink, peeling fat turnips and slicing them over a wooden bucket, with my apron hitched up into the waistline of my long, warm skirt, I looked out the window toward the creek again, attracted by some change in the atmosphere.

Snow!

It sifted down softly, everywhere, like the best refined sugar that ever was, dusting everything with whiteness, a delicate layer forming even as I looked, touching all things and making them, as the hours stretched on toward darkness, new, and strange, and altogether other.

During the last of the day, the steady, silent falling changed to a sound of howling, with eerie gusts of wind that whistled like lost boys through every crack that would let it in.

Just before dark, the mother said to me, "Take a candle, and have a look in the attic. With all this wind we need to make sure of every window in the house."

I had only been up to the attic once or twice; the thought of mounting its stairs alone, that late in the day, and with the wind making the house cry out, all but lifted the hair on the back of my neck. But I lighted a candle as she told me, and went up to the second floor, walked to the end of the hall, turned back to where the attic stairs began, and headed up, not very fast, but as bravely as I could.

Behind me, I felt the presence of the open doors and empty rooms, all those beds with nobody in them and no light except for the faint silver of their windows that would, with snow on the ground, never be completely dark even at midnight. All that emptiness and grey dimness lay between me and the candlelit kitchen below.

Ahead, the rafters above me slanted down from the low peak of the roof, high enough overhead so that I would be able to walk standing up, but at an angle far too steep to let anyone do anything near them except crouch down like a person trying to hide.

As I stepped from the uppermost stair to the attic floor, I looked from one end of the long space to the other, left and right, with the right-hand end closest. At either end, a pair of small, widely set windows, each with four little panes of glass, let in the pale, mysterious light that the falling snow created.

Between each of these two sets of windows, set away from the walls that held the windowpanes, tall black flues, the metal chimneys of stoves set far below on the first floor, carried smoke up through the roof and out of the house. Because these flues had to pass through the second floor on their way to the roof, they brought heat with them, to the second floor first, where they helped keep the girls' room and the spinning room warm, and then to the attic, so that even here, far away from the kitchen and the first-floor sitting room, I could be, at least a little bit, warm.

Straight ahead of me, across the open, planked floor of the attic, I saw long rows of drying plants hung from pegs on boards nailed across the slanted rafters that rose from floor to roof peak. Bunch after bunch, and bouquet after bouquet, herbs and other useful plants hung upside down, with their stems above and their leaves and blossoms below, drying in the semi-darkness and faint warmth.

As predicted, the wind made its way in here as well as everywhere else. The long rows of dried plants swayed, ever so gently, moved by the invisible air, like ladies dancing and bowing. I forgot my fear, and went walking from one end to the other in the fragrant,

74

plant-filled attic, making sure that the windows had remained secure. Once, without thinking, I touched a finger to a little, thick glass pane, and snatched it back as if the unexpected cold had burned me.

By this time, I could see nothing outside but a deep, cold, blue twilight, as the snow continued to fall, and the wind went on howling over the open fields. It was time to go down; I had done what I'd been sent to do, and nothing more was needed but to trot down the attic stairs with my candle in my hand, walk along the hallway past the open doors and dark, empty rooms, and then, with my back to all of that, go on downstairs to warmth and light, and the supper nearly ready to eat.

But I didn't go down. Maybe it was the thought of that emptiness. Maybe the mild, slow dance of the drying plants and dead flowers held me, spellbound, inhaling the smell of them, remembrances of garden and field and even forest, herbs grown to heal people, plants to be used for coloured dyes, to make food fragrant, to season stews and soups, to sew in bags to tuck into the storage chest, to slip under pillows, to bring sleep, to wake sleepers, to encourage dreams, to cure the colic, to bind up wounds.

As I thought of the empty fields, and the half-empty house, and the snow falling between the dark pine trees, and the silent creek, and the empty road outside, now hidden by snow, a deep loneliness crept into my bones and my heart and my thoughts.

"You are all alone," my body told me. "This is not your home. This is not your time. You are far, far away from everything and everybody you've ever known."

"What are you doing here?" my mind asked, whispering inside my ears. "Why have you come?"

I began to shiver, from standing still too long. "Will you ever get back?" my fear asked. "Will you ever go forward, to wherever and whenever you ought to be? And if you do, will it still be there? Will you, yourself, still continue to be?"

I never knew how long I stood there as the gathering gloom turned into darkness, with the rafters creaking in the wind, and the dried plants swaying in the draught, and my thoughts as cold as the snow and as deep as the arriving night.

Somehow, finally, like a person in a dream, I slowly turned to the head of the attic stairs, and found to my astonishment, somebody standing there, silent and still.

I jumped back, with my heart slamming.

"Oh! You scared me!"

The shock of it brought me to myself, as if for all that time I had been someplace else, somewhere far away.

The tramp boy, who stood there waiting for me, put out his hand as if I had surprised him as much as he had startled me.

"I'm sorry I frightened you," he said. "Most days you would have heard me coming up, but with all this wind, I can see you didn't know I was here."

"No," I agreed.

"You're wanted in the kitchen." He turned and led the way down, the polite thing to do on steep steps, I thought; if I had tripped and fallen, I would have landed on top of him, instead of the other way around.

Thinking these ridiculous thoughts, I followed him all the way down to the first floor, with my candle flaring in my hand, grateful not to have been alone in those dark and empty spaces.

"Is everything well up there?" Sarah asked me, when I came to the foot of the kitchen stairs. "What kept you so long?"

I had no answer for that, at least not one she would have understood, and I murmured something about having to check all four of the windows.

"Good girl; I'm glad you were so careful," she said, and gestured toward a basket of potatoes waiting for me to come and peel them. I took up the knife, glad I wouldn't have to explain, and glad to have something ordinary to do. As for the tramp boy, he went down to the cellar and returned with a heavy crock of pickles, which he set on a cupboard shelf to replace one that had been emptied.

"Is there anything else I can do to help?" he asked.

"No. Not for now, thank you," Sarah answered, and he went to the side door and began to put on his outside clothing.

After he left I asked her, "What brought him into the house?" Clearly, he hadn't finished whatever chores had taken him away again.

"He said he had seen a light in the attic," Sarah answered, her mind apparently on the cupfuls of flour she had begun to measure out.

"That must have been me with my candle." I pictured him, looking up and noticing the flicker of it through a window.

"He seemed very keen to go up," she continued. "It was odd, really." Setting down her cup, she gave me her full attention.

"Why?"

"He said he thought somebody up there needed help."

I couldn't say aloud what I felt, when she told me this. How could I? I couldn't tell anyone how far away I had been, until he came up the stairs and awakened me, or brought me back, or whatever he had done. I couldn't tell her how far away I always was, there in her candlelit kitchen.

But he must have understood, I began to realize. Maybe because he, too, had come very far from home, he knew what I was feeling. But how did he know he would find me upstairs? I might have been any of the sisters. We were both outsiders, I thought, then. Both of us had been strangers, taken in without question, in the middle of the night, by the family that received every guest as Christ.

After that, the night closed down so fast that we set the table in near darkness and ate by the light of several candles, the mother ladling out hot chicken broth full of rivels—flour and egg dough that I had myself helped to make—while the other girls carried out their own chores. I had rubbed the dough between my fingers until every little bit of it fell, like fat flakes of snow, into the boiling soup stock that had simmered all day at the back of the stove, with a handful of salt and a couple of onions and a crumble of dried herbs for good measure.

As with every meal, pies sat brown and heavy on the table top, and jugs of pickled beets, and a bowl of sauerkraut, and fat loaves of bread with dark thick crusts, glazed with egg and speckled with dried poppy seeds.

"Let us give thanks," the father said, and we shared the blessing, each of the eight children, and both the parents, and the tramp boy, and myself—hired girl and teacher and lost child all in one—with all our thoughts and hopes and fears, joining as well as we could.

77

Chapter Nine: Goose Quills

"Come along, now," the mother said to me, after the snow had begun to settle into the ground during a series of cold but bright days that followed the storm. "You can help me with plucking the geese, and I'll get the quills I promised, and show you how to make them into pens."

Because the creek had frozen solid and the grass around it had been flattened by the retreating snow, the geese could no longer run free as they had been able to do since spring. Instead, they waited for us in the shelter of one of the outbuildings. Every six weeks, the mother plucked the mature geese for their warm, fluffy down that kept them cozy and comfortable out-of-doors in all weathers but the coldest. Down made a light and perfect insulation, not only for the geese, who would grow more, but for us, since the mother regularly changed the down in her household's pillows and featherbeds, to keep them fresh and full.

"Hold the towsack out like this for me," she said, opening the big bag with both hands. All the goslings of the previous spring had become leggy young geese, and they came to watch, not being experienced as the elder geese.

"Hold it still, now, and try not to be afraid."

The closeness of the geese, of whatever age, made me nervous; I never got over my fear of them, with their great beaks that could deliver a punishing nip, and their wild, strange eyes, that accused us of being humans who had come to steal for our living from among law-abiding, self-respecting geese.

In spite of their opinions, the mother sat on a chair with the neck of a goose under one knee and its body on the other, not letting go no matter how it flapped its great wings and squacked its loud protests. She pulled the fluffy down away from its wide, soft breast, grabbing it in handfuls with her strong, efficient fingers.

I held out the big towsack in my scared hands, holding its top open as wide as I could, to receive the masses of fine, delicate, feathery down, with its odd animal smell, packing it in as well as I could, while stray strands of it stuck to my arms and my hair and my clothes, and tickled my nose and cheeks, and flew into my mouth so that I had to spit them out.

Afterwards, I pulled the bag closed and stood beside it, still brushing away fluff. "Are we finished now?" I asked hopefully, beginning to feel cold on this frosty morning, and wanting to get away from the bits of down that still floated in the chilly air.

"Soon," the mother promised. "But we have one more errand. You don't have to help with this. I can do it myself."

Then she leaned over and grabbed the great neck of an angry gander so fast even he hadn't seen her grasp coming. With one strong hand she swung his heavy body under her arm, and with the other hand she twisted his neck, as he squirmed and nipped and honked loudly. In a second she had broken the connection between his brain and his body. Then he sank, limp and twitching, with all his strength in ruin, and she carried him back to the house and down to the cellar. There she hung him up out of reach of mice, until he would be ready to become roast goose and be brought to the table, smelling delicious, as well as supplying goose grease in plenty, for all sorts of uses.

As I came into the kitchen, struggling to control the big tow-sack full of goosedown, she came up from the cellar, looking pleased.

"Look," she told me, and held out a handful of long, shapely feathers, plucked from the bird's powerful wings. "After dinner, I'll show you how to make these into quills."

It sounded easy, but cutting a good quill correctly turned out to be harder than I had imagined. When dinner had been served and then cleared, and everyone else had gone again to their different tasks, and Magdalena and little Sarah had been put down for their naps, the mother and I sat down at the table again. I could hear the older sisters upstairs laughing and chatting as they began to refill the pillows and ticks with the down I had brought into the house.

"First," Sarah told me, "we have to choose a quill with just the right curve. You're right-handed, aren't you?"

"Yes."

"Then you need a quill from the bird's left wing. It will have a natural curve just slightly to the right." She put a feather, that she had already chosen, into my hand. "See?"

Sure enough, it fitted exactly. I thought of the gander, flying with the help of this quill. The least I could do was make a good job of turning his feather into a good pen.

"Now, the shaft of this quill—it's called the barrel—has to be scraped from the tip, where it came from the skin. See?" The mother tapped the long, hard rod from which the two halves of the feather spread out.

"Why?"

"To take away this greasy, thin, outer skin, and also to get out the pith inside. We want it to be nice and clean."

The scraping, which I did as carefully as I could, after she showed me how, left a strong tube that I could almost see through. I held it up to the light of the window, to be sure it had been cleaned completely.

"Good! You have clever fingers," she told me, and I'm sure I blushed.

"Thanks."

"Now," she went on, "here's a little penknife. My father gave it to me. It's made just for this purpose, so don't lose it."

"Oh, no; I promise." With her help I made two slanted cuts that almost, but not quite, met at the tip of the quill's barrel, to form the pen nib, the part I would dip into the ink.

"Now, we only have to slit the nib," she told me, as if there were nothing to it. "Ink won't flow as well if the nib isn't divided."

Holding my breath, I made the tiny cut as carefully as possible.

"Now, make one more cut, across the very end of the tip. That will give you a sharp, clean point."

When I finished, trembling from having held my breath so long, I held up the goosequill pen and showed what I had learned.

"Very good," Sarah told me. "Now, what do you intend to write?"

"I want to write the alphabet, so I can teach the little ones how to do it."

"Better and better!" She smiled and took from her pocket a little bottle of ink. I recognized it as the one she used when she wanted to letter the paper label of one of the medicines she made from some of the herbs she grew and carefully dried, and pounded into powder, and placed in small glass bottles with oil or with alcohol, which she distilled from frozen cider. I had read the labels on these bottles, where they sat on the topmost shelf in the pantry, but I hadn't dared to ask how she used them: sumach, and trillium root, chokecherry root, elderberry, and gold-thread.

"Hold the pen like this," she told me, sitting down beside me and resting her forearm on the table. She held the pen between her thumb and her forefinger, resting her hand on the other fingers curled underneath.

As I took the pen and held it the way she showed me, sitting up straight and supporting my arm on the tabletop, she eased the stopper out of the ink bottle, set it aside, and placed the open bottle where I could dip into it as I wished.

"What shall I write?"

"Write the alphabet, as you said."

"Could you show me first?"

Nodding, she sat beside me, slid a small scrap of precious paper to a place directly in front of her, dipped the quill pen, and began.

The pen moved easily in her hand, tracing the beautiful shapes of the Fraktur alphabet that she had learned when she had been a schoolgirl.

"There!" she said. "Now it's your turn."

So I sat down, took up the quill, and wrote. My fingers remembered the moves because Mama had taught them to me, in just the same way, in my other life, and I remembered not to hurry.

"There," I said, when I had finished.

"Clever, clever!" she exclaimed. Then, unexpectedly, a serious expression came on her face. "Wash your quill, now, and put it away. I want to talk to you about something."

I went to do as she told me, wondering what in the world she wanted to say. When I came back from the sink, after washing the quill in a cupful of water from the bucket, I put the pen up on the shelf where I kept the books and slates and other things I used for my little pupils.

"Here is your ink," I said. "Can I put it away too?"

"It goes in the desk in the sitting room," she told me. "Mind how you open the desk lid."

With this permission, I went into the deserted room, and tip-toed to the tall desk. I pulled the desk lid down with the greatest of care, and saw, inside, to my very great interest, a stick of sealing wax, which had not been visible when I had dusted the sitting room and peeped inside. I put the ink beside the sealing wax, closed the lid, and went back to the kitchen.

When I had sat down, the mother said, "You're not as old as my eldest daughter, I know, but you will be, and—you've come from outside, as we say."

What did she mean by this? Would I find out at last who she thought I was, and how I had come to be in her household? I held my breath, wondering.

"When your folk wrote and asked if we needed an extra pair of hands, I wasn't sure. Not that you wouldn't do; you were their girl, and even though I hadn't seen you since you were a baby, I knew you would be of help. I hadn't yet written back to answer the letter, though."

She looked at me, almost like one woman to another, rather than a mother to a girl.

"But then, just like that, there you were! You came almost as soon as I'd read that letter. So I supposed she had just sent you on without my answer, because she was certain we'd take you. You came to us the very night the tramp boy came. Remember?"

"Yes," I whispered.

"And here you've been, all this time. And I'm glad of it. I thought you ought to know."

When she said that, I jumped up and hugged her, not waiting to see if it was the right thing to do. It was what my family did, anyway; what I would have done if Mama or somebody else close to my family had said such a lovely thing.

And it must have been right, because she made us each a large cup of tea, pouring boiled water from the kettle over dried scraps of mint leaf and setting the green brew in front of us. Taking up her own steaming cup, she sipped it. Then, "I have something to tell you that I think you ought to know."

I held my breath.

"You need to understand about the tramp boy."

"Yes?"

"He's not—one of us—not a Mennonite."

"No." And neither was I, I thought anxiously.

"So his ways aren't ours," she continued.

I waited silently.

"And it seems his master—the man who has come here—isn't his master after all."

"No." I agreed. "I heard him say that, in the barn."

"So you already know?"

"I already know that, but nothing more."

"That man had stolen him away, and made him serve as an apprentice, though he'd already become a journeyman, and should have been allowed to work for himself."

"Yes! I knew that too. How could somebody do that? Why didn't he just tell people what had happened?"

"It seems he had his reasons."

"What, then?"

She pressed her lips together, as if she didn't want to say any more. Then, "He'd been half-starved, for sure," she said, "and roughly used as well, by the look of him."

I remembered his bruised shoulders, and found I couldn't speak.

"But he's a brave youngster," she went on. "Rough handling wouldn't have held him when he could have slipped away at any time. It's what the man said that kept the boy by him."

She shook her head, and I could see anger in her blue eyes. "He told the poor lad that his mother would be killed if he didn't stay and serve out a second apprenticeship."

"That's terrible!"

"So it is. And the boy stayed, believing it, until one day he realized that the man had never truly met his mother, and had no idea where she lived. He'd been so frightened and hurt, and so weakened and bewildered by hunger, you see, that he'd never thought clearly about it, until…."

"Until what?" I couldn't stand another minute without knowing.

"Until his false master decided to move from Pennsylvania to Canada West, to our village here in Waterloo County, where we

Mennonites came half a century ago." She shook her head slowly, thinking about that. "If all these folk that have come here since had been like him, what would we have done?"

"The man has settled here?"

"We're not sure. But he has certainly taken lodging, so my husband says, over the tavern that's up on the hill. That's how our tramp boy got away. The man had made him sleep in the stable to save the cost of a room."

"Selfish creature!"

"Well you may say so, but it proved to be his best chance. Another tramp sheltering there told him about our Mennonite ways, about the beggars' rooms, the tramp rooms to be found in our farmhouses. And he set out along our road in the middle of the night, and came to our door, to strangers he'd been told would take him in."

"Poor thing."

"Poor, he may be. But he's not afraid of work."

"No," I agreed.

"We'll keep him as long as he needs us," she continued, "but he'd be happier earning his own way by his skills, if only this man would let him be."

"Why won't he?"

"I suppose because he still hopes to profit from him."

"It's hard for him to have to keep hidden."

"It's hard for us, too." She put her hand, red and chapped from work and weather, into the pocket tied under her apron, and pulled out a crumpled bit of newspaper, already yellowing. "Look at this!"

She held it out to me, and I took it, cautiously, as if it might burst into flames in my hand, laid it on the tabletop, and smoothed it out with trembling fingers. It proved to be a tiny advertisement, printed in German, its Gothic print jumping from the page:

Attention!

Runaway apprentice, sighted in the neighbourhood.

Excellent reward when returned.

It gave a man's name, and the name of the tavern where he'd taken a room.

I had seen that tavern on one of my visits to the village when I had taken the little sisters to school. It must have been a handsome inn in its early days when people came along regularly by coach and on horseback, as they once did in great numbers. But when I saw it, it had grown shabby. The wooden walkway in front of it had become broken, so that we all looked down at where we put our feet when we walked past.

A stink of stale drink had breathed out of the half-open door, and the stable, visible down a short lane at its side, gave out a breath of decaying manure and rotting hay, which nobody bothered to clear and clean, leaving the stalls dirty and the horses' mash to spoil. Living on a well-kept farm had taught me to recognize bad management and neglect.

"This man could have us up before the law," Sarah said, bringing me away from these thoughts.

"But he's not his true master."

"We've no proof of that, though I believe the lad's story."

"What are you going to do?"

"We haven't decided."

Why had she told me all this? To warn of trouble to come? To be able to talk to somebody outside her family, outside her community, maybe?

She said no more, but drained her cup of tea. It must have become cold as it waited for her to drink it. She went to the stove to stir up the embers inside; the kitchen had grown cold, too, while we sat talking. Frost glittered on the window; wonderful patterns had formed there, but they gave me no comfort.

I stood up too, went to the pantry for a broom, and began to sweep the kitchen, not the first or the last of my chores for that day. Doing a quiet, careful task calmed me, and set my mind free.

I had formed an idea, a secret idea. But I would need help to carry it out.

Chapter Ten: Candle Making

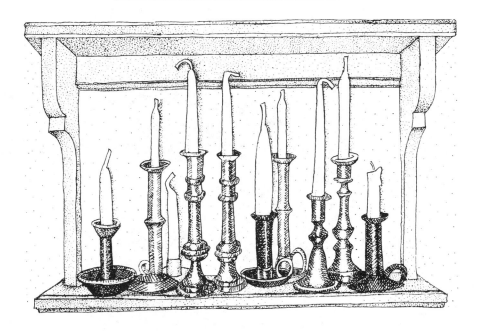

At that time of year when the snow had already fallen once and would surely fall again, the days seemed to shorten faster than they had when the bright leaves blazed on the trees and the sun still had its power to warm. We saw the sun sometimes, even now, but sunny days had become the coldest days, burning our cheeks and making our fingers ache, even indoors.

During this darkening time, the mother called all of her girls, including me, into the kitchen.

"Time to make candles," she said.

She had the tallow and the beeswax heating already in one copper vessel inside another large vessel of boiling water, steaming away on the stove top.

I thought about beeswax and tallow. What a lot of trouble it must have cost the bees, to make sweet-smelling brown wax out of their own bodies, in order to form the combs that held their honey. It smelled sweet even now, though all the honey had been taken from it and it had been heated and strained to make it clean and pure. The older sisters used beeswax to polish the wooden furniture in the sitting room. Their mother heated the wax with a little turpentine, then cooled it to a soft, fragrant paste. Being trusted to polish everything perfectly made them eager to do this careful job.

Tallow came from animals too, from sheep suet, as the mother told me, though beef suet could be used too. She saved the suet, a kind of solid, hard fat, and rendered it in a black pot, taking care that it poured out clean and pure, and letting it harden. Tallow made not only candles but soap; somebody had to stir it out-of-doors as it boiled over a fire set at the same spot in the yard where the family made apple butter. Mixed with lye made by leaching ashes with water, tallow became brown soap that washed us clean and stung our eyes. Like beeswax, tallow too could be used for polishing. Somebody had to rub all the leather parts of the harnesses and reins with tallow to keep them supple and strong. I had seen the tramp boy at this task.

"What are you dreaming about?" Sarah asked, waking me from these thoughts. "Here, take a turn. I'll show you how."

She had laid out strands of linen string and the older girls had begun to tie them to metal rods, which they set above blackened racks of candle molds, rows of cylinders set up straight, exactly candle-shaped. Each mold had a string hanging down inside.

"Watch," she said, and she filled a dipper with melted candle-wax and poured precisely enough into each waiting mold. "If it smokes, its too hot," she told me.

"How long do they take to set?"

"Longer than they ought, to curious minds," she answered. "Watched pots never boil, and watched tallow never sets!"

All the girls giggled; I knew they had been told this themselves, more than once.

"Come and help me, while you wait," Barbara beckoned to me, and I went to the other end of the table where she sat. "You can help me cut more wicks."

Carefully, we measured out more lengths of string. "Come along to the stove now," she said.

Handing me one piece of string, and taking the rest in her own hand, she led me there, and showed me how to dip each of our wicks into the waiting tallow, dipping, letting the wax set, and then dipping again. After many careful repetitions, a full taper had formed, longer than the molded candles.

I tried to follow her example, and gradually learned how to judge how long to let the wax set after each dipping, and how many times to dip each taper to bring it to the perfect size. We worked mostly in silence, as we repeated our motions in a kind of rhythm. She had now for the first time treated me almost like an equal, though I was surely at least four years younger than herself.

I could hear the younger girls murmuring and giggling with their mother and Mary; somehow I knew a moment had come that needed to be caught before it could fly past and be gone.

"Barbara," I whispered, "could you help me with something?"

"What?" She looked at me in surprise.

"I need to send a letter," I told her, "but I don't know how."

"Oh." Her face brightened. "That's not hard. I can take it to town for you, and post it." She had understood; I wanted to send a letter in privacy, and she had agreed.

"I can't pay for it," I said. "But I'll do anything I can to thank you."

"That's all right," she said, smiling. "I can manage the price of a stamp."

I couldn't keep my plan completely secret, of course, in a family full of sisters. The next morning, Lydia came to me, as I sat up in bed and swung my feet over the edge of the mattress.

"Teacher?" she said, looking up with her blue eyes gleaming.

"Yes?"

"Here's a present for you. Lizbet told me to give it."

She held out a single sheet of clean paper, ready for whatever I wished to write on it.

I took it from her small hand, a precious gift. "Thank you."

The child smiled and walked away with the sigh of a person who had carried out an important assignment, her fair braids hanging neatly down her small back. I had my paper now, and I knew what I wanted to write. Even so, the hardest task would be next.

I waited my chance very carefully, watching the tramp boy come and go. We seldom spoke; he spent more and more of his time with the father and the brothers, as they finished one by one the tasks that needed doing before the snow fell and stayed fallen. As he went about his business, I saw that he had already grown taller; boys of his age shot up in jumps, apparently. The trousers he had been given now showed his ankles, and his frost-reddened hands had been joined by exposed wrists, as his shirtsleeves crept upwards day by day.

One morning, just before breakfast, I went to the henhouse for eggs, and, coming out with them, I saw him.

"I need you to tell me something," I said.

His eyes opened up like moons, and I saw a pulse throb at his throat, but he stood still, his hands at his side, and waited.

"I need to know where you come from."

He looked at me intently, for so long that I thought he wouldn't tell me. Then, softly, he answered, "I come from Pennsylvania."

"Where in Pennsylvania?"

Again, he paused. Then, he named the town.

"Now, I need to know your mother's name."

"Why?"

Could I lie to him? Would he guess my plans? Would he believe me if I told him? Finally, I stammered, "I—I just wondered. She must be missing you, mustn't she? Wondering where you are? She doesn't know, does she?"

"No," he said, more sharply than I had ever heard him speak.

I was afraid to ask more, afraid he wouldn't talk to me again. Then, as I had almost given up hope, he spoke her name, in a voice almost too soft to hear.

As I stood repeating that name and the name of her town, again and again in my mind, so as not to forget them, he walked away. Holding the eggs, I went to the side porch, and, out of the wind, set the egg basket down and felt in my pocket for my piece of paper, which I had carefully rolled up, and for a pencil stub that I had saved from my morning task as a teacher. I wrote the name of the tramp boy's mother on my paper, along with her town in Pennsylvania, and put it back into the pocket. Then I went indoors with the eggs. All the rest of that day, my hand went to that pocket, feeling the paper roll to be sure it hadn't been lost.

At night, before I fell asleep, I planned what to do when my chance came, and, in the mid-afternoon of the next day, when everyone else had something to do outdoors or upstairs, I found myself alone in the kitchen. The low sun had moved well along on its shallow arc across the sky, and looked into the pantry window, leaving the kitchen in shadow, not dark enough to need a candle, but enough to make it seem lonely.

Holding my breath, I tiptoed into the sitting room, where nobody went on a weekday without a good reason.

There, I walked through the open centre of the room, with a certainty that somebody would come immediately behind me, or would spring up outside one of the windows and peep in to catch me at my secret task. I could hear the tall clock ticking, and I felt the chilly air of the room, away from the kitchen stove, and with its own small stove unlit and cold.

As I crossed the floor toward my goal, I repeated again in my mind the words I intended to write, and at last I reached the place I wanted to be.

There I stood, in front of the largest piece of furniture in that space. The tall, beautifully made, red-stained desk, with its many dovetailed drawers precisely fitted into their waiting places, and its hinged desktop closed at a shallow angle, rose up and looked back at me, every part of it firmly shut and not expecting to be opened.

As if the rose-coloured wood of it might burst into flame at my touch, I slowly put out my hand, and in one motion took a knob and lowered the desktop. It went down flat and ready without a whisper, easy as one could please. Even so, doing this without permission seemed much harder than doing it when I had been told.

There, waiting for me to choose them, lay the prepared goose-quills, as I knew they would be. And the little pot of ink sat there too, with the light of the frosty afternoon window glinting from its surface.

I held my breath, spread out my roll of paper and pressed it down until it became flat, unstoppered the ink bottle, took up a quill, and began to write. I paid so much attention to my task that I forgot to listen for anyone who might choose that moment to walk into the room.

Because of the hour, or because of luck, or as Mama would have said, Providence, or because of what I was doing—I never knew which—nobody came. I finished my letter, and wrote the tramp boy's mother's name on the outside, along with the name of her town. I took up the piece of sealing wax that I had seen there before, and then, I realized my mistake.

I hadn't remembered to bring in a candle! Sealing wax wouldn't melt by itself, and without the wax, my letter would not be sealed; everybody would be able to open it up and read what I had written.

"Drat!" I whispered, and almost jumped out of my skin as the clock suddenly broke its forgotten ticking with a grind and a rattle, and a single "Bong!" as it sounded the quarter hour. With the sealing wax in one hand and the letter gripped between my teeth, I closed the desktop with the other hand, and ran back to the kitchen with my heart hopping up into my throat.

There, too, I found nobody, and I stood still, trying to recover my breath and my wits. When I dared, I lit a candle and set the candlestick on the table. Then, as carefully as I could, I softened the end of the hard little stick of sealing wax, and pressed a melted dab of it onto the back of the folded letter, where one end lapped over the other. Listening for the least sound, I made three little pools of hot wax, one in the middle, and one at each end, and, lacking a seal, I pressed each small puddle flat with the candlestick's base, adding splashes of candlewax to my letter in the process.

Finally satisfied that the letter wouldn't be able to fly open without somebody to break its seals, I set the candlestick aside, blew out its flame, and looked at my handiwork. Not very neat, I told myself, but good enough to survive the trip to Pennsylvania, or so I hoped.

As I put the letter in my pocket, I heard somebody on the side porch, and realized that I still had the stick of sealing wax clutched in my free hand. Just like a child, I put that hand behind my back, and looked up to see Barbara, coming in with an armful of wood.

"Is everybody else still upstairs?" she asked.

"I—yes."

"Good." She picked up the kettle and leaned over the stove to poke up the coals inside. "Let's have a cup of tea."

Then, as she turned back to look at me, she broke into a grin. There I stood with one hand still in my pocket and the other holding up the sealing wax, with my mouth hanging open, wondering what to say.

"Finished with your letter, have you?" she asked.

With a great sigh of relief, I took the letter from my pocket and handed it to her. She accepted it, and without even glancing at the words I had written on the outside, she tucked it neatly into her own pocket and set the kettle over the newly awakened flames.

"Go and put the sealing wax away," she said, and I scampered off to do what she told me, coming back to find her reaching into a crock for a handful of dried mint leaves to make mint tea, and to hear her mother's footsteps coming down from upstairs.

"Making tea?" Sarah began. Then, with the mind-reading instinct of all parents, she looked at me and at Barbara, and said, quick as a wink, "I think I've forgotten something," turned around and went up the way she had come.

As soon as she disappeared, Barbara took my hand. "Sit down, now, and be at peace. I'll take your letter with me tomorrow when I go to run errands. It's my day to go to town. You can come with me, once you've given the little ones their lessons, if you like, and prove to yourself that I've sent your letter safe and sound."

"Oh, yes, please," I answered. "Thank you!"

We set out the cups and she poured the boiling water onto the mint, so that when her mother came down again with the rest of her daughters trailing behind her, we were ready for a rest and a drink of hot tea, and a visit before we began to make supper.

As I sipped at the tea, holding my cup in both hands to warm them, I looked out the window at the front of the house, and gazed away east toward the darkening sky. The trees at the far side of the fields across the road had become completely leafless long since, and they huddled together, naked and grey, while the shadow of the farmstead reached out across the frozen fields, as if it wanted to follow those trees into the night.

We had lighted the candle, and its light grew brighter and the stove burned more warmly, as we all sat together, contented with each other's company.

Chapter Eleven: The Spinning Room

The following week, all of the girls in our house gathered in the upstairs sitting room, the spinning room the family used in the fall; all except for the two littlest ones, whose busy fingers could not be trusted near the spinning wheel. Spinning flax was difficult and that job usually went to Barbara, whose hands, the most experienced in the household except for her mother's, had begun to spin the flaxen fibre into the yarn she would need in order to have linens for her dowry. A weaver in the nearby village would weave the yarn into sheets and towels and other linen things. But every pair of hands could find something to do in the spinning room, and every tongue would wag at the same time.

The flax fibre we had so carefully made now hung like a shining waterfall from the tall wooden distaff attached to the side of the spinning wheel, which crouched in the centre of the room on three outspread wooden legs. Light poured into the room set in the northeast corner of the second floor, its door opposite the girls'-room door at the front end of the hall. It brightened the pale grey walls and green woodwork, and shone on the ochre painted floor, where we had gathered our small painted chairs and footstools, and sat in a circle, keeping our spinster company, and taking our part in meeting the family's textile needs.

With her skillful hands, Barbara drew down fine strands of flax fibre from the distaff to the whirling spindle. The wheel began to revolve when she rocked the wooden treadle with her foot. A steady, musical hum sounded as the wheel whirled and the thread formed in her fingers became a fine strand that shone like pure gold, soft and smooth and extremely strong. I could see the twist of it, a pattern faintly visible on its glistening surface, and knew that a second thread, whose twist went opposite to the first, would be plied with this one to form a fine, strong linen yarn that would not unravel. At her side a large wooden reel was ready to receive her finished work.

As she sat quietly spinning, the rest of us took out our various tasks and began our work too. Lydia sat on a little stool, and pulled from her pocket a scrap of linen cloth, a small brass thimble, and a precious needle that she had carefully threaded into the cloth for safekeeping. Next came a length of linen yarn that her mother had cut for her to use. This, she licked with her little pink tongue. Then she held up its end in one hand and the needle in the other, and tried to put the thread's end into the needle's eye.

I had to clasp my hands together to keep myself from threading it for her. I knew she needed to learn how for herself.

"Teacher?" she asked.

"What?"

"Can you help me?"

"I—of course. You have to be sure your thread comes to a point. Here, let me show you."

I took the damp thread's end, and, pinching it between the thumb and forefinger of one hand, I pulled it through with the other. The yarn came out flat and more inclined to being put through a needle's eye.

"Oh," my little pupil said. Up went the thread point, and the next second, in it slipped, as neatly as could be. She pulled it partway through, but she made no knot. "Thanks."

With a satisfied smile, she set to work on her bit of cloth, turning one of its edges over once, then twice, to become a hem, and forcing her needle in and out along the folded edge with her thimbled finger. She would do this, I knew, until her mother had pronounced these stitches to be perfect. Each time she finished a row, she trotted out of the room and pattered down the stairs to find her mother. Each time she did this, I could hear the interested chatter of the babies who were down there, helping their mother in their own way.

On her third try, she came up with her face shining. "Look!" she cried, and displayed her hem for everyone to see. "Mama says it is 'very good work'!"

Everyone stopped to admire the row of little stitches, including my other pupil, Louisa, whose stitching had already reached the approval stage.

"Very good," Louisa said, in an exact echo of her mother.

Each of the girls had a small willowsplint basket, with sewing needles, knitting needles, spools of thread, balls of yarn, thimbles and darning eggs, couched in nests of sweet-smelling curls of unspun wool which reminded me of the thirty sheep that Sarah kept. I had seen their fat, round bodies dotted about a field near the house when I first came, but they were stabled and warm for the coming winter, now; Joseph and his sons had sheared them, and had put by many sacks of greasy wool for the summer, long since washed and spun and put to use. These little curls of clean fleece had been kept for stuffing quilted things that needed to be especially thick and warm.

While Barbara spun her flax into yarn, with a happy and intent expression on her face, Mary took out her wooden darning egg, held it by its short, spindled handle and pushed its smooth cheek into one of her brother's knitted woollen stockings, threaded a large needle with woollen yarn, and began to mend a gaping hole in the stocking's toe.

"What in the world does he do, to wear these out so fast?" she complained. "Surely I mended this only last week."

"Maybe he does it on purpose, just to give you something to do," Louisa joked.

After that, Louisa knitted quietly, making a sock to be worn and darned in its time, and all of us worked in a mild silence as the spinning wheel whirled on.

In one corner of the room, a large basket sat waiting, with used clothes ready to be mended. Some of the clothes would be cut down and altered to fit the younger children, or cut into squares to stitch together to make comforters that were stuffed, tufted with yarn, and used to make warm coverings. Some of the scraps would become stuffed toys; dolls, maybe, or ducks and dogs and cats. I had been sent upstairs more than once to add to this pile of outworn dresses and threadbare trousers, waiting to be patched or mended or recycled as long as anything at all could be made of them.

While the others worked, I took up my basket too, and began to make a little pocket of linen cloth. I cut a piece twice as long as it was wide, folded it half across its narrow width, and stitched up each side, leaving open the edge opposite the fold. Then I turned the whole thing inside out so the raw edges wouldn't show, and filled it with loose wool, like a sort of sandwich. Then I carefully turned the edges of the opening in, and sewed them together, as neatly as I could, hoping that when Sarah saw my handiwork, she would approve.

Finally, I began the task of quilting through the layers of cloth and wool, to hold them together and keep the filling from bunching up together and leaving some parts empty. I quilted rows in both directions until my work had a diamond pattern with all its lines as straight and its stitches as small as I could make them. This very practical labour produced a quilted hot pad, to keep somebody's fingers safe from a heated pot or kettle.

While we sewed, we started chatting again, and then began to sing, quietly, in concert with the humming wheel. From time to time, Lydia dashed away to consult her mother about her practice stitches. Then, as her feet came pattering up the stairs one more time, I heard her calling out.

"Hush!" I hissed, and the others stopped singing. Even the wheel fell silent; Barbara looked up as if she had wakened from a happy dream.

"Somebody's here!" Lydia called out, scampering down the hall. She trotted through the doorway, and added, "Mama's not down there."

By this time we could hear a fist knocking heavily on the front door. My heart began to pound; I remembered my first night in the house.

Then Barbara stood up, alarmed, and just as she did, we heard the sound of hurried footsteps from the back of the house downstairs. As the hammering on the door continued, somebody came up the stairs, moving extremely fast. I thought I recognized Sarah's tread. By the time she burst through the spinning-room door, we were all on our feet; she had baby Sarah on her hip and little Magdalene by one hand, with her cheeks flaming and her cap strings flying. Behind her, his face white and his eyes enormous, came the tramp boy.

Handing the baby to Barbara and Lena to me, Sarah leaned over the basket of worn clothes, and began to toss out an apron, a cap, a petticoat, and an old dress of her own, for our waiting hands to catch.

"Quick! Put these on him!"

The tramp boy tore off his shirt and rolled up his trousers, as Sarah handed out the girl's clothes to the rest of us. As fast as we could, we helped him struggle into this unaccustomed clothing. Our fingers were clumsy with fear and shyness, but we managed to get him dressed.

Slim and young, he made a passable girl, with a cap on his head to hide his shorn hair, and his stocking feet—he had kicked off his boots somewhere outside—tucked under the hem of his long skirt.

"Sit there," Sarah told him, pointing to where I had sat. Sitting there among the rest of us, only his strong, large-knuckled worker's hands—the hands he used to earn his keep and make a living—could give him away. The mother draped a shawl over his lap to cover them, and took my basket of sewing to hide them still further.

Grasping my hand, she led me with her to the top of the stair.

"Do you feel brave?" she whispered.

"Not very."

"You must try," she said, "because I need you to answer the door for me."

"Why?"

"The boy's false master is there. He's never seen you, and you can say that you're the hired girl, if he asks. Tell him that you don't know much about the family. I know that couldn't be true—hired girls always know everything, and tell it too, sometimes—but maybe he'll believe it; he doesn't know our ways. Now, go!"

And down the stairs I went, too scared to think about the consequences. As I descended, the knocking stopped. I tiptoed to the door, reached out, shot the bolt, and lifted the latch, pulling it open like somebody in a dream.

Peeping around the edge of the door, I looked up into a cold, sharp-featured man's face.

I had never seen him before, and he had never seen me. I stared up at him, a tall man in a dark, tailored coat with huge patches of sweat under the arms, and he gazed down at me, his yellow teeth bared in the midst of his trimmed black beard.

"Well, girl," he hissed, "have they left you alone at home?"

I knew better than to draw back; he wanted to see weakness. I stood still, gazing upwards, at his soiled silk tie and his once-starched collar, wilted from long travel and bad lodgings. The smell of him, hair oil, tobacco, and male anger, poured out between us as I stood, and the cold air from out-of-doors poured in too.

"I'm here," I said, as steadily as I could. "But the men are close by. They'll be coming for a meal, any time now."

"And is your mistress in the house?" he asked, more mildly, when he heard that.

"I'll call for her."

"Never mind," he said. "I can look for her myself."

He took me by the shoulders and set me roughly out of his way. The grip of his fingers scared me more than anything I had ever experienced. He moved me aside like a chair or a door, like something to be shoved out of the way, and broken, into the bargain, if he had cared to take the trouble.

As he came into the kitchen, his sharp eyes swept its space, empty of everyone but us.

Did I glance at the stairway? Did I make some move, some sound he could interpret? Could he smell them, upstairs, breathing out fear? Whatever told him, up the steps he went, with me behind him, his boots hammering on the treads for everybody up there to hear.

When he reached the topmost stair, a tiny sound came along the hall, the chirp of a little girl's voice, silenced too late.

He strode along the hall toward the spinning room, and I knew they would hear him coming. The mother met him at its door, the baby in her arms.

"What do you want here?" she asked, in a voice as cold as stone.

I didn't wait to hear more, but dashed down the steps and out toward the barn; the father met me as I came.

"He's come, the bad master!" I gasped, and he went by me, running.

His sons came out of the barn behind him, and we all ran then, with me last, out of breath, as the long legs of all of them outran me. The boys stumped onto the side porch, leaning over to pick up thick sticks of kindling, and I struggled ahead, up the stairway to find the father, his face dark above his beard, facing our unwanted visitor at the very doorway of the spinning room.

"What do you mean, coming up here among our womenfolk?" he asked, in a voice to match his wife's.

"No harm intended," the man answered, in a soft voice that sounded the way his hair oil smelled, so sweet and false it made me sick to hear it. "Surely I've a right to search for my stolen property."

"There's nothing here of yours," Joseph answered.

"Maybe not." The intruder stood there, glancing at the room of girls, as he clearly thought us to be, with the look of one to whom females of any age were of little use and no importance, except to meet whatever needs he might have had.

Then he turned on his heel, strode past Joseph and past me, too, as I shrank out of his way, my shoulders still aching from his grip, and my lungs sore from my running.

Down the stairs he went, with a tread fit to break every step, and strode out the front door, slamming it behind him.

Peeping down, I saw David and Samuel, each with his stick in hand, at the foot of the stairs, just too late to catch him. I crept downstairs, and Joseph followed me, stepping firmly and without hurry.

"He's gone, child," he said to me. "You needn't tremble so."

Then he saw his boys, with their eyes like saucers.

"Put down your weapons, my sons," he said, in a quiet voice. "You know that's not our way."

Sarah came downstairs, then, leading her little ones, and the older sisters followed her, looking here and there as if the man would still be hiding somewhere. I suppose we cried, if not outwardly, at least inside, because our house that had seemed so sheltering and safe, had not, as it seemed, protected us.

Last of all, the tramp boy came down, too. He walked slowly, like a person exhausted from long travelling. He had changed back to his usual clothes, making him into his own boy self again, with his ill-fitting shirt and trousers, and his hair pressed down by being kept under a girl's closely binding cap.

When he saw us he broke into a sudden grin. "How can you stand all those tight fitting things?" he asked us; maybe he had seen our sad faces. "Layers and layers! I thought I would smother!"

We all giggled, as much with relief as with his joking. "He didn't see you at all," I said. "You were just one more girl to him."

He answered, more soberly, "Such clothes make a good disguise, it's true." He turned his gaze to the mother, who stood at the stove; I knew she had been listening.

As he looked, she turned toward him, and put out her hands. "A man like that is everyone's enemy," she said. "I'm glad you escaped him."

He let her clasp his hands, looking into her eyes. "You saved my life," he told her.

"You are not a child," she said, as if she were speaking to herself as much as to him. "I see that, now. I'm sure I can find you better fitting clothes than these, let alone the ones you wore just now. Come, we'll look in the spare room."

Then, as we all stood staring, she led him up the stairs, saying over her shoulder as she went, "Set the table now, my dear ones. See how low the sun has gone."

We all went about this work at once, glad of a familiar thing to do, and began to carry plates and cups and all that was needed, from the cupboard to the table, laughing together from sheer relief. Outside, the sun, low enough to peep directly through the pantry window, shot a sudden beam slantwise across the kitchen, touching the floor with its light.

Chapter Twelve: Peace Cookies

As November moved toward its last days, and more and more of our chores had to be done in darkness, overcast days found us at work indoors in a daylong twilight, so dark that we had to burn candles if we wanted to see our sewing. The kitchen now felt like heaven, and we brought our work there and sat near the stove or at the table, glad of such light as came in the windows. Then, as we knew it must, snow began to sift down again, and the reflected snowlight filled the room.

"Today we'll begin to make cookies," Sarah announced, just as I had finished my morning task as a teacher, and my pupils had gone outdoors to play in the newly fallen snow as a reward for paying attention. She took baby Sarah, who had been playing with Magdalene on a mat just far enough from the stove to keep them from being burned, and just close enough to keep warm.

"Up, now, my darling!" Tiny Sarah sat on her lap, chubby and contented, with her short legs straight out and her little stockinged feet stuffed into small woollen booties padded with washed fleece to keep her toes as warm as possible. Her cheeks, like those of everyone in the household, had a bright red glow from being chapped by the cold. Her mother kissed her on each of these rosy cheeks and on the tip of her tiny nose as well, and then began to sing:

> Hop, hop, hop, hop,
> Rider mine,
> Like a little
> Sun, you shine!

As she sang, she bounced the little one on her knees, and at the end of the verse, she raised the baby especially high, calling "Hop!" and brought her down to a chorus of giggles and squeals. Little Lena kept time by clapping her hands.

Then, with a last hug before setting small Sarah on her feet to walk away to where she had been sitting, the mother turned to me as I sat with Barbara and Mary, who had put their sewing down and begun to chant the hopping song along with her.

"Now, let's get started," she said. "Call in Lyddy and Louisa."

Outside I could hear the shouts of my two pupils. The light snowfall had dusted the frozen grass with a spangled layer, and as

I went out to the side porch I found them dashing back and forth, making snowballs with brightly mitted hands, only to see the balls come apart as they flew, scattering white powder over their knitted shawls. The wings of their bonnets flapped as they ran, and their skirts flew up about their ankles, showing their quilted petticoats.

"Come in!" I called, clasping my shoulders with crossed hands as I felt the sharp air of the out-of-doors. Their squeals continued but their game brought them up the steps, and as the last bursts of snow flew from mitted hands and shawl-covered backs, into the house they came, and stopped side by side as they spied their mother standing in her long apron with a big wooden spoon in one hand and a large, brown-glazed bowl in the other.

"Which of you wants to be first?" she asked. "We're making cookies."

"Me! Me!" they called out in chorus.

"Put away your shawls, then, and come help."

The girls hurried to hang up their snow-dampened shawls, and placed their wet mitts in a row on the bench that stood underneath with its back to the wall.

As soon as they could, they scampered to where their mother stood.

Looking down at them, she smiled. "Christmas will be here before you know it," she said.

Hearing that, a memory of my own mother came galloping back, sharp and intense as a knife to the heart. I saw my family in my mind, decorating the Christmas tree, with myself and my brothers hanging up the ornaments, and Mama on a chair putting the angel on top, and Daddy making approving noises after he had helped to string up the lights.

But even as I trembled with pain at these memories, I knew that the Schneider family would never have had Christmas trees. Even in my own century, the conservative Mennonites kept to the old south German and Swiss customs in which the Christmas tree had no place. But cookies were definitely a part of their Christmas.

Turning to her waiting daughters, Sarah continued, "You can choose which cookies you want to make."

Barbara, smiling contentedly, waited for the others to reply.

"We'll make peace cookies!" Lydia and Louisa cried.

Their mother, who had obviously guessed what they would say, turned to her cupboard and took down a basket full of metal objects. When she sorted them out on the scrubbed tabletop, they became a row of metal shapes, formed into birds, prancing horses, moons, suns, and stars, open hands, and two different sizes of hearts.

"Cookie cutters!" I exclaimed. Cookie cutters they were, and I watched with delight as the younger girls carefully chose from among them, taking turns, the shapes they wanted to use.

Then Mary announced her choice: "I'll make Saints' Hearts!"

At last, Barbara spoke. "I'll make peppernuts," she said, and her mother smiled, as if they shared a sweet secret.

"What about you, then, Lizbet?" Sarah now said to me.

"I'll make peace cookies too," I replied. I knew I'd be able to use the metal cutters for them, when the little ones had taken their turn. Cookie cutters reminded me of Mama, who collected them, and said, every Christmas, "Life without cookies is not worth living!"

"Good, good," Sarah agreed. Then, her eyes dancing with fun, she added, "How shall we begin?"

They all knew the answer to this, and as I waited to see what would happen, all of them, except the eldest, trotted into the pantry and brought out the maple sugar, made from maple syrup that had been boiled until it crystallized.

Before anything else, the maple sugar had to be broken in pieces and pounded into a loose powder that could be mixed with sifted whole wheat flour, fresh butter, and cream of tartar, measured out carefully, in combinations according to the different recipes.

They also brought out a crock of apple molasses, which would give its own dark tang and deep colour.

"Come, you can make the spices ready," Sarah told me. "I'll show you how."

Leading me to the pantry, she took down the spice box, a finely made wooden container shaped like a cupboard lying on its back, with a sliding lid. Carefully, she pulled the lid along its pair of grooves, and there they were—many spices, sorted into small square compartments. A fragrance came out like the smell of Paradise on the world's first morning.

One by one, she pointed to each compartment, naming the spices it contained, and as the day went on, she showed me how each one had to be prepared, after its own kind, and carefully measured with the right spoon or cup.

Whole cloves, shaped like spring flowers, that smelled like spiced cookies all by themselves, needed to be pounded flat until they came apart into a coarse powder, unless they were to be poked whole into soft dough to form the spicy eyes of cookie animals.

Nutmeg, which looked like small brown nuts, had to be grated on a little tin grater made just for the purpose.

"Watch your fingers," Sarah warned. "It's easy to grate them at the same time."

I held the nutmegs carefully, and as I rubbed each one down the prickly little grater, they formed a delicate dark powder with a magical smell.

"Very nice," she said, and we both inhaled the rich fragrance they gave.

Pieces of ginger, dried and strangely shaped, like gnarled and twisted fingers, I also grated, to make a spicy seasoning that burned my tongue when I touched a damp finger to it and brought the pale gold shreds to my mouth. I made a face when I discovered how hot it tasted, as if I had taken a burning coal into my mouth!

Anise seed, tiny, dark rod-shaped forms smelling like licorice, needed only to be measured out, but the black pepper, used for making peppernuts, had to be ground in a pepper mill carefully carried from its place on a shelf, and held over a little bowl as the black and grey fragments fell like dark rain, making me sneeze.

Last of all, came the lemon, yellow and precious and rare, bought at the little greengrocer's shop in the village, where such things, like the big dimpled oranges, could be seen at this time of year. It had to be grated too, spilling fragrant strips of bright yellow rind into a pile like summer snow. After its beautiful outer rind had been taken away, the mother carefully rolled the white pulp-covered lemon again and again between her hands, and then, setting a tiny sieve over a cup, neatly cut off one end and pressed out the pale, deliciously sour juice, along with a remarkable number of seeds.

When all of us finished this part of our work, a row of shining brown bowls of carefully measured and mixed dough sat on a shelf in the coolest part of the pantry, which was very cool indeed, each smelling sweeter and more fragrant than the last, waiting to be rolled out flat with a heavy wooden rolling pin on a flour-dusted cloth spread upon the tabletop. All except for one bowl. This, the dough prepared for peppernuts, had to be rolled into little balls between the palms of Barbara's hands.

"These will keep for a year if I put them in a closed tin," she told me.

When their portions of dough had been rolled, the little girls took turns with the cookie cutters, pressing the various forms into the dough, lifting the cut pieces up ever so carefully, and setting them in rows on the blackened metal trays.

I waited my turn until only one bowl still held a ball of peace cookie dough.

"Teacher's turn," my pupils announced.

Each hopped up into a chair and leaned over to watch.

"I have an idea," I told them. "Are your hands clean?"

They held up their flour-smeared hands to show me. I heard their mother chuckle; she came to the table to watch as I carefully rolled this last ball of dough until it lay out flat and smooth.

"Now, you first," I said to Lydia. "Put your hand down on the dough, but don't push. Good. Now, spread out your fingers."

She held very still, looking serious, and with a blunt knife I carefully traced around her fingers until a small hand had been cut into the dough.

"Now, where's that little heart?"

"Here!" Louisa lifted up the smaller heart-shaped cookie cutter.

I took it, and, very carefully, pressed it into the palm of the hand we had formed. Then, with even more care, I slid the flat spatula under the hand shape, so that it came up with the heart shape still in place.

"Watch, now," I told my audience. I laid the cookie hand onto a waiting tray, and then pried out the heart and set it in a place of its own. Now the hand still had a heart in its palm but it was a heart's shape, made clear by its neat edges, even though its dough had been taken way.

"My heart and hand," Sarah said, softly.

Barbara and Mary had come to watch. "This means 'friendship,'" I told them.

"Not 'I give you my heart'?" asked the bride to be.

"That, too," I said, and we all laughed.

Then everybody took a turn having their hand shapes cut into dough, and having the heart shapes cut away and set beside them. After that, the task of baking began.

The barrel-shaped oven could be opened at either end, and a cookie sheet set carefully in place inside, left to bake, and then taken out again, by careful hands, protected by homemade hot pads, including the ones I had made myself. The kitchen began to smell so sweetly of spices and baking dough that we sang the table song about the Lamb's Table.

All this kept us busy for hours, broken only when we served dinner, and finished just in time to make the evening meal and scrub the table clear, while the oven was kept hot by a steady fire, heating a large pot of soup, set away to the side, simmering, for most of they day. Now, Sarah ladled bowls of it for the table. Bread made yesterday and kept wrapped in linen towels, bowls of sweet and sour pickles, cups of fresh milk and hot coffee, a bowl of left-over clabbered cream poured over boiled potatoes seasoned with dill seed, and a mound of sauerkraut in a bowl of its own; all these found their way to the table.

As we placed the last tray of cookies in the oven, darkness, which had crept across the windows without our noticing it, filled every corner of the kitchen.

"Light another candle, would you?" Sarah asked me, drying her hands on her apron.

As she said these words, we hear the sound of boots on the side porch, and hurried to finish before the family's menfolk came into the kitchen.

"What do I smell?" Joseph asked, with a chuckle that told us he knew that cookies had just come out of the oven.

Lydia and Magdalene ran to him and clung to his long legs as he stood at the pantry door, admiring the plates of cookies we had assembled there.

"Who made these?" he asked, and each of the makers answered in turn as he admired each plateful, one after another.

"And what did our baby do?" he added, as the tiny Sarah jumped up and down hoping to be picked up.

"Ate cookie dough!" Magdalene told him.

"Dough! Dough!" little Sarah echoed. He leaned over and swept them both up at once, holding them one on each side in his arms.

At that moment, Barbara darted from the pantry back to the kitchen. "Something's burning!" she cried, and pulled open the oven door with her bare fingers, placing them in her mouth to be cooled, and then snatched up a hot pad and rescued the last batch of cookies, setting them across the dry sink where they would become cool enough to touch so that she could lift them off onto a waiting plate.

As Joseph and his flock of cookie makers returned from admiring their day's work, and Sarah had finished setting out all the dishes and cutlery, their brothers came in, having washed their hands in a bucket of warm water their mother had set out for them, and leaving their boots on the porch. The tramp boy entered last, looking changed and more grown up in the new clothing Sarah had taken from the spare room storage chest for him.

After we sat down and asked the blessing, the boys ate with a mighty appetite after their chilly chores. As people who had spent our time tasting cookie dough, we girls could eat more slowly, and with more dignity. Sarah smiled at her brood, passing the bowls and baskets as needed but eating, I noticed, like a person who had also tasted her share of sweet dough.

When we had all finished, we stood up, and the boys and their father left the kitchen, followed by the tramp boy, while the girls began to clear the table. As I picked up a couple of bowls in my turn, the mother touched my arm and took me aside.

"Could you do something for me?" she asked. "I think I forgot to close the molasses barrel this afternoon when I went down cellar. I don't want to dip up a drowned mouse the next time I need to bake."

Of course I went, taking up a candle from the table. Holding it out to light my way, I went slowly down the cellar steps, as the smell of cold stones, damp bricks, and ancient earth came up to meet me, along with the smells of winter vegetables, smoky sausages, and wooden kegs. As I tiptoed carefully from tread to tread, one hand out to touch the wall, and the other supporting my candle, I began to hear soft voices.

I stopped where I stood, not so much for fear as from curiosity, and blew out my candle so as not to be seen. I saw the faint light below, showing that a candle had already made its way down cellar before me. I stood perfectly still, trembling with indecision, wanting and yet, not wanting, to overhear.

"I can't stay," the tramp boy said. He spoke in a low voice, but I could hear him clearly. He sounded firm and determined.

"You are welcome here," Joseph's voice came.

"I've no right to endanger the women of this house."

"You can leave protecting them to me."

"I could get away, I'm sure; I'll go tonight, in the darkness. Then everyone here will be safe."

"You'd be throwing your life away," Joseph told him firmly. "And I won't be a party to that."

"He knows I'm here; I'm certain of it. Every day he becomes more sure."

"How can he know?"

"By the way we've all behaved, not going to town alone, leaving somebody here all the time." The tramp boy named all our careful precautions. "He watches us; I've seen him. He walks by every day, staring into the windows."

"That's true," Joseph mused. "But he's seen nothing. We always go and come from the house in the dark."

"He can tell which of us I am, at least when I'm dressed in my own clothes. He knows the shape of me well enough."

Joseph let out a long breath, like a sigh. I had the feeling this was not the first time he and the tramp boy had held this conversation. "Stay, boy," he said, after a silence. "We need your help."

Though I couldn't see them from my place on the stairs, I knew that the father had won. Without speaking, they began to walk toward the foot of the steps; I heard the tread of their feet on the brick floor, and I backed up hastily, all the way into the darkened pantry, and waited for them to come up into the kitchen and move away, so that I could slip down cellar alone and make sure the barrel was properly closed. I had to relight my candle, but I managed to compete my task without being seen.

When I, and my many candle-cast shadows, found the barrel, its cover sat neatly in the place carved out for it on top; it had been closed all the time.

Then I understood why I had been sent there, and, up in the kitchen again after bravely turning my back to the cellar's absolute night, I found the mother putting away the last of the washed plates, and spoke to her.

"He's decided to stay," I told her.

She gave no answer, but she touched my hand with her work-roughened fingers, and smiled.

Chapter Thirteen: More Visitors

W hen the snow came to stay, it fell quietly, blowing sideways and sifting into every crack and crevice.

"Here it is," Sarah announced, to nobody in particular, as she stood in her kitchen. I heard her speak as I came downstairs in the morning, and I went to join her at the window as she looked out. "I'd say this time it means business," she told me.

It continued all day and all night and all the next day, until a hard small sun like a knot of pure gold showed itself late in the afternoon as it moved down its low arc, casting a huge blue shadow from the farmstead across the fields that would lie flat and white and frozen all the way to spring. The naked trees and dark pines cast their own long shadows to match.

Wrapped in my shawl, I struggled to the well, with a bucket in my aching hands, to fill it for supper. The frost, though it had turned the top of the earth to iron under the cover of new snow, couldn't reach down far enough to freeze the water in our well. But the creek had disappeared, like everything else, under the snow's cold blanket. My leather-shod feet squeaked on the white hard layer that covered our brick path, making me afraid of slipping, and making the handle burn my fingers through my knitted mitts.

After I drew up a bucket of water, I stopped to look at the cold sun's light, and at the long shadows it cast. A cloud of steam formed from my breath as I stood there, gazing. Then, as I turned toward the house, I could see past it to the road, which came downhill from the village to pass before our eastward facing veranda.

Looking up the hill where the road went north, I saw the huddled buildings, houses, and steeples, every roof white and smooth, with streamers of grey smoke rising straight up, now the wind had stopped, into the empty sky, not a blue sky, but a sky silver with ice crystals, deepening toward sunset even as I stood there, shivering.

Along the road, a figure came, slowly, somebody tired and worn at the end of a long, long journey. Something held me there, watching. After a time I knew the person for a woman; she carried a traveller's bag on her arm, and moved carefully, placing her feet into the packed snow, step-by-step, not quickly, but steadily. I could see her face as a cold-stung pink oval, and her dark shawl over her head and around her shoulders. She was no girl, but she carried herself, tired as she seemed to be, erect and firm, moving forward with purpose as she came.

I knew, with sudden certainty, that she could see me, too, and as her face became clear to me, I began to walk forward, set the bucket on the side porch, went along the side of the house, and met her at the gate, as she stood there hesitating and gazing up at the front of our well-built Georgian house.

Looking into her eyes, I knew I was not mistaken. "You are our tramp boy's mother, are you not?" I asked. Then I called her by name, and she smiled, a smile I already knew from the face of her son.

"He's here, then?" she asked, her familiar face alight. "He's safe?"

"For now." As we spoke, I lifted the latch and pulled the wooden gate open. "Let me carry your bag; you must be worn out with so much travel."

She gave it to me, and it swung down heavily in my hand. Taking her by the arm, I walked up the front path at her side, and we mounted the wide veranda and stood before the tall, grey, many-panelled door.

She lifted her gloved hand and knocked, and the door swung open so quickly I knew we had already been seen from inside.

The tramp boy stood there, his face ablaze. He took his mother into the house and into his arms, bending his face onto her shoulder.

"Mother," he whispered.

I had to look away. A sharp cold flash of loneliness shook me, and I carried the bag inside and took my place with the others; the mother and daughters of our household.

"She's his mother," I explained, though nobody would have doubted it. "I'm sorry, I left the bucket on the porch when I saw her. I'll go fetch it."

I hurried outside so no one would see my tears, and, after drying those tears on the sleeve of my dress, I picked up the bucket and brought it, already feathered with loose ice on its surface, into the welcoming warmth again.

"Sit down, sit down," Sarah greeted her visitor. She gestured toward the sitting-room door. "Let me take your shawl. Come in; be welcome."

Everyone entered that special place, and sat down on the many chairs as if this day were Sunday.

"Bring a cup of tea for our guest," Sarah said to Barbara, and, turning to me, she added, "Call in the men, if you would."

Out I went into the cold again, glad of the errand, and walked as quickly as I could through the snow to the barn, where I found Joseph and his sons in one of the stables, mucking out straw. The sharp and familiar smell of manure hung in the air, and the breath of animals and humans steamed up in clouds, though the bitterest cold kept away from this half-underground place.

Joseph stopped working and stood erect, the pitchfork in his hand and a look of wariness on his face.

"What's happened?" he asked, before I could say a word.

David looked at his father, and Samuel looked at me; each had a question in his eyes, but neither of them spoke.

"The tramp boy's mother has come," I told them. "You're needed indoors, if you please." I turned and walked back to the house without waiting to see what they would do.

I heard them following, their boots crunching and squeaking in the hard-frozen snow, and, after they had left those boots on the side porch, we came into the kitchen.

"They're here," I said.

They stood in a row, the two boys trying not to stare, and Joseph gazing at the matched faces of the mother and her son. Thrusting out his big, work-worn hand, he clasped the hand of his visitor, and she returned his gaze with a great dignity and calm.

"You are welcome in this house," he told her.

"I am glad to be under your roof," she replied.

A sudden silence, broken only by the ticking clock, settled in the room. Then, "How did you come to look for your son here?" he asked—the thing they all wanted to know. The tramp boy glanced at me, and to my astonishment, he gave me a conspiratorial wink, looking more like a boy of fifteen, as I suppose he must have been, than he had looked all the while he had stayed with us.

125

Then he sat down in a chair beside his mother, took her hand, and waited to see what she would say.

"I had searched everywhere for him, when he didn't come home from his apprenticeship as I expected. I went first to his master, of course, and was told that he'd gone off with his new clothes and his carpenter's tools and apron, and the master's good wishes for a safe trip home and a job awaiting him there as a journeyman. I followed the route my son had planned to take, but"—she glanced at him—"he couldn't be found. Nobody had seen him, it seemed, one lad among so many."

"Where had he been sent to be an apprentice?" the father asked.

"To Philadelphia. We were lucky; his master is a good man, and a capable teacher. His cabinetmaking is as fine as may be."

"You had seen his work?"

She smiled faintly. "He was my brother-in-law. I kept a few of his first pieces after my husband died; they had been wedding gifts to us. They've lasted well; they were well made by my judgement."

This brought a thoughtful silence; her son sat up straight, as she spoke, like a person accustomed to beautiful furniture.

"Then, where did you look?" The father pressed on, "You kept on hoping surely?"

"I hoped, but it became harder. I had almost given up, when the letter came."

"The letter?" he asked, and Sarah turned suddenly to me, with a gleam of understanding in her eyes.

I clasped my hands together in my lap and stared at them, praying not to blush.

"Your letter. The one that came addressed from your town with your name on it. Why do you ask?"

She reached into a little bag that swung at her waist, pulled out a crumpled piece of paper, smoothed it out carefully upon her lap, and held it up.

Everybody stared at it, of course, except the tramp boy, who gazed at me with an expression so intense that I had to look away.

"That came from here?" Sarah and Joseph said, almost in chorus.

"Did you write this?" Joseph asked his wife.

"No." She turned to me. "But I think I can guess who did."

Everybody looked, as I sat there, wishing to disappear. Nobody spoke.

I stared at all of them, at the faces that had become so familiar to me. They sat so still, waiting for my answer, that they could have been a group in a family photograph or portrait, caught in a frozen moment of time.

Somehow I found the courage to speak. "I wrote it," I said. "I asked him for his mother's name and for his town, not so big a town, I hoped, that word of the letter wouldn't come to her one way or another."

"The postmistress told me about it when I went into her shop," the tramp boy's mother said, nodding.

"How did you go about sending this letter," Joseph asked me. "You never left the farm; at least we told you not to go."

At this, Barbara raised her hand. "I mailed it," she explained. "I had permission to go to town."

Her father looked at her like a person seeing someone for the first time. "So you went on an errand of your own?"

"I took it along when I was sent to get something at one of the shops." The room became silent; nobody spoke, waiting, I suppose, to hear what Joseph would say.

Up popped Lydia, and chirped out happily, "And I gave teacher a piece of my paper so she could write her letter on it!"

The whole atmosphere in the sitting room changed after this. Everybody smiled and sat more comfortably on their chairs. Joseph turned to me again, and asked, "What did you say, then, in this letter? With so many helpers listening, you'll tell us, surely."

"I told her where her son was staying and gave the name of our family, and our address. At least, I gave the name of our village and how to find our farm. And I explained that our tramp boy had been taken by a bad man who posed as his master, and had been held captive through a threat to kill her, if he didn't stay and do as he was told."

I saw a look of dismay on the tramp boy's face, as I went on talking. "And I told her how he had been treated badly, how he had—had...."

I couldn't bring myself to say any more, and I couldn't bear to look at the tramp boy, either.

His mother leaned across and took my hand. "All that's over, now. We are together again. We'll go back home to our town and be safe there. I've never met that man, and unless my son has told him where I live, he can't know; we lived a long way from where he apprenticed, even though we have kinfolk there."

"I didn't tell him where you were, mother, because he didn't ask," the tramp boy said, then. "He had told me he knew where to find you, that he had friends who would—would harm you, if I left him."

The father, who had listened carefully to my confession, and to these responses, now spoke again.

"You did well," he said to me. Then, turning to the tramp boy's mother, he added, "Your son will make a good man. He hasn't forgotten what he learned from his true master, or from you, so it seems. He's been a great help to us these past months, and more than paid his way by his work. Even so, it is true that he's been in danger."

He stopped speaking, and looked at Sarah.

"His false master is nearby still, in the town," she said. "He has tried at least three times to get hold of your son and take him away again. You may not be able to go to your home as safely as you hope."

"If I can get back to the railhead, we should be safe," the tramp boy's mother said.

"Of course; you came by rail! We are living in modern times!" Sarah exclaimed. "Was it—was it very expensive?"

The woman smiled. "Not considering what I came to do." She looked at her son, who sat very still, his shoulders back, and his eyes fixed upon her face. "I sold a few things, in order to pay for the trip."

"What things?" the tramp boy whispered.

"Some of your master's work. He knew; he understood."

This, of all he had heard, brought to the tramp boy's face the deepest look of sadness. He shook his head, slowly. Then, "I'll make them again for you, I promise, when I have a shop of my own."

"I know you will," she answered. "All in good time."

"So, then," Joseph said, "You came from the railhead to the village by coach?"

"I did; a very rough ride, with snow falling. I had to take lodging for the night before I could continue. And then the coach left at midday. But I came as quickly as I could."

"You are welcome to stay with us," Sarah said. "You need to rest before you travel again."

"I can't trouble you further; you've already done enough, keeping my son safe."

"It's no trouble! Stay, do; we'll have supper ready soon. It will be dark before you know it. You can go tomorrow, or the next day, whenever you are truly rested."

Joseph held out his hand; "When you do go, I'll take you to the railhead myself, in our cutter. A sleigh will make a smoother ride and a faster, too, now that the snow has fallen."

Mother and son gave him bright smiles, then, and Sarah reached out to take his hand.

"Come, let's get ready," she said, and all her girls stood up, including me. Then, she turned to her guest. "Please, take this chance to visit with your son. He has first rights to all your news! We'll hear more later, when you've rested."

Then, just as we rose to go into the kitchen, somebody began to pound on the front door.

Chapter Fourteen: The Christkindl

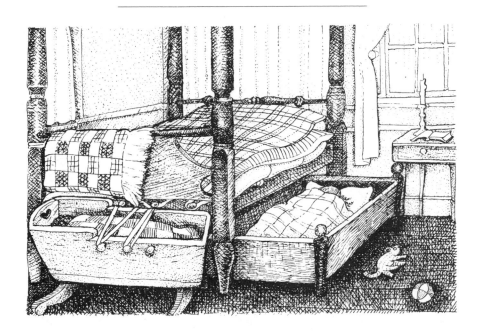

The faces of the tramp boy and his mother went as pale as milk. He made a sound, low in his throat, more like an animal in a hunter's trap than any sound a human could make, or so I would have thought if I hadn't heard him.

"Stay here," Joseph told us.

We all sat, frozen and speechless, as he rose and strode from the sitting room to the kitchen, and swung open the veranda door. I couldn't bring myself to look, and as I turned away, I saw the anguished recognition in the tramp boy's eyes as he looked past me to see who had come.

"You are not welcome here," I heard Joseph say.

"That's no matter to me, sir!" the false master retorted. I would have known his voice anywhere. "I'm here for my property."

Then I heard another voice, one I could not recognize. "That's as may be." A man spoke, in a deep rumble.

I turned and looked, then, in spite of my fear, and saw, framed in the doorway, a tall policeman. Certainly, he looked like a policeman, red-faced, closely shaven, and big enough to discourage argument. I had been told that not all tramps were welcomed in the town, and that local laws could be enforced against them.

"Come in," Joseph said, in a voice warm with relief. "You're welcome here, certainly."

When these men had entered, Joseph closed the big door, and all three of them stood between that door and the stairs. As they paused there, Sarah stood up and joined them.

"Sit down," she said, in the same voice she would have used to stop her sons from scuffling, and in a wink all three men had seated themselves at the kitchen table. "You'll take coffee, surely, on such a cold day?"

Embarrassed baritone murmurs answered her, and she set to banging away at the stove to bring its embers alight, and filled the kettle with a splash from the pail in the sink, where I had put it.

While she carried out these domestic acts, the three men spoke to one another, so stiffly that it might have hurt them to say their words.

"You have something of mine," said the false master.

"I have not. All those in my protection are free persons; nobody is a slave in Canada West," Joseph replied.

"He's my apprentice; I have a paper to prove that he's bound to me."

"Show it, then," the tall man rumbled, and the false master pulled out a roll of paper from the inside pocket of his coat and opened it on the table.

At this, the tramp boy's mother arose, and swept across the sitting-room floor. From the bag at her waist she too pulled out a roll of paper.

"I am the boy's mother," she said. "Here is his lawful contract, already fulfilled."

She unrolled it and held it up. "Look; here are the signatures, master and apprentice. And here are the dates, the day he entered his true master's service, and the day he left as an acknowledged journeyman."

Joseph took this document from her and held it open on the table with one strong hand at each end. "Put the other beside this, and we'll see!"

The big man leaned down and looked, passing his fingers from line to line, as people did whose reading wouldn't come easily.

"The signature on your paper gives the same name as the other, ma'am," he said.

"But they are not written in the same hand," she told him. "Look again."

"That is true," he agreed, after a careful check.

"It's a trick!" the false master roared.

"What about this?" the tall man asked.

"That's easily solved," said the tramp boy's mother. "Let him write his name for you, and then compare the two."

At this point a big pot of steaming roasted-barley coffee thumped onto the table, and Sarah began to pour out scalding coffee into three cups. "Will you have milk or cream?" she demanded.

Nobody answered her.

"Let him write, then," growled the false master.

With a sigh, the tramp boy's mother beckoned to her son, and he came, his face like chalk, with his head erect and his shoulders held back bravely.

"We need a pen," Joseph said, and I dashed to bring a quill, along with the ink. By that time everybody knew that I knew where to find them, after all.

"Here," I said. I unstoppered the bottle and placed the quill pen in the tramp boy's fingers.

He began to write, leaning over and carefully forming his signature, each letter beautiful and clear.

"There," he whispered.

And of course, his signature matched the one his mother had brought.

The false master reached out to snatch away the true certificate of apprenticeship, but the tall man moved his great hand as fast as a striking snake, and grasped his wrist.

"Hold back," he commanded, as the false master twisted in his grip.

"You know you signed for me!" the angry man shouted. "You've falsified your own signature! That's an offence in itself! I'll have you up before the magistrate!"

Calmly, the boy looked back at him. "I did. I admit it. But you forced me to it."

He placed his hand, with its knuckles down, flat on the table before them all. There in his palm, his old scar gleamed like a star in the silver light of the late afternoon, made bright by the reflection of the low sun on new snow.

"This is your work," he said. "You set my own chisel there, and pressed its point so deep it cut the flesh. You said you'd drive it through my hand, into the table, and I'd never work for any master, if I wouldn't sign. So I wrote my name as you told me, but not in my own true signature."

In the silence that followed, everybody looked at his hand, at the scar the false master had left there.

"Maybe you should leave now," Joseph suggested. "You have business elsewhere, surely."

The man stood up, his face gone purple. "You'll see me again," he hissed.

"I don't think so," the tall man told him. "Unless you really do want to see the magistrate. We have strict laws against the use of subtle craft in this county. I'd be glad to show you the very statute, if you'd care to come along with me."

"No, thank you," said the false master. "I'll be on my way. As has been said, I have business elsewhere."

He rose, went to the door—the door that nobody but strangers ever used—opened it, and let himself out, leaving it open behind him with the bitter cold air pouring in to blow away the evil smell of him.

After a silence, Sarah closed the door, and locked it. "There," she said.

Then, as if nothing at all had happened, she continued; "Won't you all have coffee now? Or tea, if you like. The kettle's still hot." And she went to the pantry and brought out a plate of the cookies we had made from where we had stored them, wrapped in cloth, in covered bowls.

Everyone came into the kitchen, then, young as well as old, and sat at the table.

"See if the babies are in our room, would you?" Sarah asked me. When I went through the pantry and the storage room, there the little ones were; Magdalene lay in her trundle bed fast asleep with her thumb in her mouth, under a small feather tick, while baby Sarah lay snug in her cradle, with her own tiny coverlet covering all but the curls on the top of her head. They had slept through everything.

I knew they'd be unlikely to sleep again at their regular bedtime unless I wakened them, so I woke each one in her turn, took away the baby's damp underclothing, splashed them both with water from the basin, and sent each one in fresh underthings, warm clothes, and little booties, to find their mother and sisters at work preparing supper.

As I settled the little ones in their favourite place on the bench near the stove, with a cloth toy for each one, the tramp boy's mother came into the kitchen. Seeing us there, she came to me and took my hand.

"I thank you for my son's life," she said. "That man would almost certainly have killed him, after he'd finished making use of him."

"I only—I only wrote the letter. I'm glad it got to you and that you were able to come."

"I'm glad too. But if you hadn't written, I am sure he would have been lost."

"Everybody here helped to protect him. Your coming made it certain."

"I came because you wrote," she said. "And we'll never forget your help."

"Thank you," I said. "I'll never forget you, either."

Everyone stayed indoors that evening, as the sun slipped behind the dark horizon and night came, cold and starry after the two-day snowfall. Mother and son visited, answered questions, told each other all they had seen and suffered, and became acquainted with each other again. The older girls sat wide-eyed and even open-mouthed, listening without a sound, and the sons, while pretending not to listen, heard every word too, as they sat with their big hands folded on their knees and their eyes fixed on the ceiling, which they examined with the greatest care. Joseph listened too, more openly, and asked a gentle question now and then. I also listened, and Sarah at her work at the stove moved so silently that I knew she could hear the conversation too.

We shared a long and satisfying supper, stretching it out longer than any since I had come to that house, until at last the father rose, and beckoned the boys to their last chores. He glanced at the tramp boy, and would have gone out without him, but the boy stood up without an invitation, and went out too, ready to lend his hand to their tasks. As he went, the two brothers stepped apart, and he walked across the kitchen between them toward the side-porch door.

Very late, certainly much later than usual, I stood in the kitchen, yawning, looking about to see if anything had been left undone.

"You'll come up, surely?" Sarah asked when she found me there after some last errand in the cellar, fighting her everlasting battle against mice, as I supposed.

"Yes. But I'd like to stay here a little while, somehow."

"Don't forget to damp down the stove, then, before you come up."

"I won't forget."

"You've been a great help to us," she said unexpectedly.

"Thank you. You've been a great help to me, too."

After she went away through the pantry toward the first-floor bedroom, I sat there alone in the darkness, lighted only by a glow from the stove, as starlight shone into the kitchen, and their beams, reflected from the glistening snow, made the whole room faintly visible.

I thought that the household had all gone to sleep, including the tramp boy's mother, for whom a bed had been made up in the spare bedroom upstairs. Then, I heard a footstep on the side porch, and a tap on its door. Tiptoeing to the window, I peeped through to see the tramp boy, with the light of the stars on his face, waiting quietly to be let in.

Cold air came in with him, so icy I could hear trees creaking and ice cracking, ever so faintly. Then I shut the door and followed him across the kitchen to the table.

"Here," he said softly. "I have something for you." He patted the back of a chair, and I sat down.

"What is it?"

Slowly, he drew from inside his shirt a small object wrapped in paper. "This is for you," he said. "I've finished it at last." He began to open the paper wrapping with a faint rustle.

Holding my breath, I put out my hand, and with the greatest care, he placed a small, perfectly carved wooden figure there.

I cupped it in my palm and lifted it up, as carefully as he had done, to see it by the starlight pouring in from the window, my night vision now fully awakened.

"It's—it's an angel?" I asked. "It's beautiful!"

"Not exactly an angel," he replied. "It's a *Christkindl*—a Christ Child."

"Baby Jesus? To put in a manger? Where are His swaddling clothes?"

He smiled, gently. "Not a Baby; a Child. Tonight is the Eve of St. Nicholas. I'm sure you know who St. Nicholas is."

"Of course. He comes to bring presents to children."

"Yes. But he's not the only gift bringer."

"This is surely not the *Belsnickle*—the one who brings switches and coals to naughty children."

"No," he answered, with a laugh. "Certainly not. Look closely. What do you see?"

I gazed at the carven figure that lay so smooth and perfect in my hand.

"This is a beautiful young boy," I said. "He hasn't any wings, but there's a crown on his head, and he's holding out his hands like somebody giving a blessing, or bringing a gift."

As I spoke, I began to shiver, maybe because the stove's fire had finally burned down to a bed of sleeping coals; maybe because, as I looked into the little carved face, I caught a glimpse of somebody I knew, or used to know, or hoped to meet again, someday. I shook my head.

"I'm beginning to fall asleep," I said. "Sorry."

"Maybe you should go to bed. I'll walk up with you."

Suddenly I understood.

"This is what you were carving, out in the barn, that day, isn't it?"

"I've been carving it ever since I came here. I meant it for you, all the time."

"Thank you. Thank you! It's beautiful. It's the most beautiful thing I've ever seen."

As I stood up with the carving held in both hands, I suddenly leaned over, without thinking about what I intended to do, and kissed him, brushing the corner of his mouth with my lips.

"Come along now, little sister," he said softly, and, as I walked up the stairs, he walked up too, behind me.

"They've made my bed in the spare room tonight," he whispered. "I'm not a tramp boy any more!"

"Goodnight, then," I answered. "See you in the morning."

Then I went along the hall, past the empty tramp room, which opened darkly at my side, toward the front of the house. I stood there, looking out the hall window across the fields. A pale light reflected from the great sweep of fresh snow that covered them all the way to the black border of bushland at the horizon, where, next morning, a fresh new sun would rise up gleaming in the east.

Standing still made me realize how cold the house had become, and I went into the girls' room, where my own bed waited for me.

Chapter Fifteen: St. Nicholas Day

W hen I woke up, I felt stiff all over. I turned to reach for my coverings, which had somehow slipped off in the night, and then, not able to find them, I patted the place where I lay, and felt the cold, hard, smooth-painted floor.

I sat up with my head swimming and a sense of shock all the way to my toes. I had fallen out of bed, I told myself. Sure enough, there I sat, on the floor of the girls' room, at the farthest side away from the door.

Spreading my apron out over my long rumpled skirt, I looked for my shawl, and found it in a heap, pushed aside, I decided, in my sleep. I felt extremely stiff and sore, as if I'd spent the whole night there on the floor. With an effort, I stood up, waiting until an unexpected dizziness passed, and, finding my cap at my feet, leaned over to pick it up, and then stood again and replaced it on my head. I rubbed my hands together to make them warm, and then, crossing my arms, I tucked my fingers under my armpits to get still warmer.

Little clouds formed in front of my face as I stood there, breathing out warm breaths in that icy room. I began to shiver in spite of being fully clothed.

I tiptoed carefully to the doorway, and peeped out into the hall. The silence told me that I had indeed been left entirely alone.

As I paused, I turned to look out the window at the end of the hall, where it overlooked the road. But all I could see, peering through the frost, was a pair of tall, full-grown evergreen trees, overshadowing the house and hiding the view of that road completely. Still mystified, I turned away from the window and walked into the spinning room. There, as I looked past more frost-flowers toward where the village should have been visible in the distance, I saw the buildings of a large city, just beyond the creek, and I understood.

"I'm back," I whispered. "This is my own century again."

The family, the sisters and brothers and mother and father— and the young journeyman and his mother too—all had gone, far away, into the past. As I stood there, understanding, tears formed at the corners of my eyes, and I felt a deep sense of exile and loss.

Then, I left the spinning room, walked along the upstairs hall past the empty and silent tramp room, turned to the top of the stairs, and went slowly down to the kitchen. Everything there shone and gleamed in the early sunlight, which peeped inside wherever it could through the sparkling frost on the windows.

The kitchen lay absolutely silent, too, so still I could hear my own heart beating, and the sound of my blood singing in my temples. I'm all alone, I thought. There's nobody here but me, now; nobody but me.

Then I heard footsteps, firm and determined, coming along the side porch. I dashed to the door to pull back the latch and all but fell into the arms of the first of two people who stood there, looking astonished.

"Mercy!" Mama exclaimed, as I threw myself against her, hugging as if I would never be able to let go. "What on earth are you doing here? I thought you said you were going to Malinda's house!"

"I was, but...."

"You haven't spent the night here, have you?"

Stepping back from my hug, I looked at her, wondering what to say. Then, "I have, that's right. I've been here all night. But...."

"But nothing; what's happened?"

"I'm not sure, Mama. I think I fell asleep while the storyteller was entertaining the children. I must have slept all night, but I'm not certain. What day is this?"

"St. Nicholas Day, of course. Are you sure you're all right?"

"St. Nicholas Day?"

"Yes. Last night's party celebrated St. Nicholas Eve. We have it here at the historic house every year," she explained, in her teacher's voice, as if I somehow wouldn't remember. "Are you sure you're all right, darling?"

"I'm fine. I'm just—confused. Let me think. Yes, I forgot to tell Malinda's mother that I could come to her house for the night. So I guess she went home without me. I hope Malinda's feelings weren't hurt."

"If she didn't know your plans anyway, I'm sure it was fine," said Mama. "And since I thought you had gone with them, I wasn't worried either. If I'd known you'd spent the night alone here, that would have been a different matter!"

Now the other woman, whom I recognized as the museum's curator, spoke. "If you've got all that straightened out, come along, both of you. I think you'll both enjoy what we're going to see."

We followed her along the porch which had been enclosed with glass to keep out the weather when the house had been restored, and went into the museum wing, where we mounted the stairs to its upper floor, and went toward the curator's office.

"What made you come into the historic house, Mama, if you really meant to come up here?"

"It's funny. I don't know. We both told each other we ought to have a look to see if it had all been put to rights for today."

"And had it?"

"Evidently. We found you, didn't we?"

The curator, who had already gone into her office and sat down in the chair behind her desk, said, in a voice become all business, "Sit down, now, and let me show you what we've got."

She unlocked a drawer in her desk and pulled out a small container made of the white acid-free cardboard that museum conservators used to protect very old and precious things, and set it in a place she had cleared on her desktop. From another drawer she plucked out two pairs of white cotton gloves made especially for handling historic objects. Then, glancing at me, she took out a third pair, and handed two of these pairs to us.

"Put them on," she said, though Mama had already begun pulling hers over her fingers, and I struggled into my pair too.

With her own gloved hands, the curator carefully opened the little box, and took out a small packet enclosed in bubble wrap, opening this in its turn. Finally, she pulled away a layer of acid-free tissue paper, and we saw what she had.

I gasped, and then covered my mouth with my gloved hand.

There, placed on the desktop, in a nest of tissue paper, lay a little woodcarving, a perfect *Christkindl* with his beautiful face, his delicate crown, his young boy's body in its simple costume, and his bare feet positioned so he could stand, if set upright. He held out his hands, in the gesture, palms up and open, of a person who wanted to give us something.

In the palm of one carefully carved hand, I saw a tiny cut, or dent, as if the carver's chisel had slipped. Or rather, I knew, with a sudden certainty, as if the point of the chisel had been driven into that upturned palm, sometime, somehow, somewhere.

I couldn't speak. I could scarcely breathe.

Mama, however, asked the curator excitedly, "Where in the world did you get this? It's absolutely magical! Who made it?"

"We've just acquired it. The acquisitions committee agreed it would be perfect for our collection. You know what it is, of course."

"Of course! It's a *Christkindl*, the loveliest I've ever seen," Mama answered.

Then I found my tongue. "Do they all look like this?"

"Oh no," said Mama. "The *Christkindl* can be a little baby angel with a halo and wings, too."

"Like a cherub or cupid?"

"Sometimes. People used to hang them low down on the Christmas tree, to overlook the gifts laid out on Christmas Eve. Trees were put on tabletops, then."

"And what else could the *Christkindl* be?"

"It could be a tall lady angel, with a crown on her head and a golden dress and outspread wings, like the ones on top of Christmas trees; people still have figures like that even nowadays."

"We have one."

"Yes. And sometimes, the *Christkindl* can look like a pretty little girl, walking in the snow, carrying presents and lighting candles on a forest pine tree. In other pictures, she is a helper for St. Nicholas, and they both come walking through the snow to bring presents to children."

"And sometimes they look like this one?" I longed to hold the figure, to take the precious thing into my hands again.

"Yes. Like a wonderful young boy, like the Christ Child, growing up in Nazareth, getting taller, and learning what his parents had to teach him."

"And this kind of *Christkindl* is a gift giver, too, right?"

"To me, he's the loveliest of all."

I agreed, but I didn't trust myself to speak. Inside, I felt a great upspring of secret joy.

"So," Mama said to the curator, "Do you have an attribution? Do you have any notion who made this?"

"We certainly do; we can't believe our luck! This piece looks exactly like the work of the '*Christkindl* Carver'," she replied. "He lived and worked in Pennsylvania in the third quarter of the nineteenth century; he's best known as a superb cabinetmaker, especially in the later years of his career, the very last period that anybody made furniture of that quality in his community. Not many pieces are known, but they are clearly recognizable as his work, and those that have been discovered are breathtaking."

"And he made *Christkindl* figures on the side?" Mama asked.

"That's what we believe. Again, not many have been found, but the ones that have are very much prized."

"Our committee didn't go to Pennsylvania, surely?" Mama asked. "I thought we kept to Canadian works."

"That's the amazing thing," the curator exclaimed.

"This showed up in Ontario?"

"Yes! Most unexpected. It appeared in a local auction, actually— our committee attended it because a rumour suggested there might be some artifacts from our own historic house's original owners. It didn't seem likely, but we had to go see. And then this turned up!"

"Well," said Mama, "I can see why we needed it for the collection. It fits right in, even though I suppose it must be a Pennsylvania piece, since it matches the others. Maybe somebody had brought it here when they moved to Canada, or something like that. It's perfect for our annual Christmas exhibition."

I could hardly wait to leave; I was about to burst with what I needed to tell Mama. But I had one thing to ask before I did.

"Could I—may I hold it? Please? I'll be careful."

"Sure. Hold out your hand," the Curator said. "Keep it over the desktop, and don't drop it." And, with care, she set the precious carving into my gloved and upturned palm.

When I closed my fingers around it, like a jewel enclosed in a flower, I felt, even through the cotton glove, its smooth carving, its delicate form. And it wasn't cold. Somehow, it felt as warm as if another person, only a moment ago, had taken it, just then, from a pocket against his own body, where he had put it to keep it safe until he gave it to me. I knew who had made it, and I knew it had been made for me.

"I'm glad you've found it," I said. "It needs to be kept safe, and it will be safe here. I'm sure it's happy to be home."

Mama and the curator smiled, though they had no idea what I meant.

Then I placed the perfect *Christkindl* figure back into its nest of paper on top of the desk.

"Can I come and see it sometimes?" I asked, hoping not to cry.

"Of course. You'll still be a junior interpreter, won't you?" the curator answered.

I nodded, unable to speak.

As we left, with further thanks from Mama for having been invited to see the new acquisition, she and I walked out of the museum door, and went slowly down to the creek through lightly falling snow, and waited at the wide city street that passed in front of the historic house until the pedestrian crossing looked safe, and at last got into her Volkswagen in the big lot where visitors were allowed to park.

"You recognized that *Christkindl* figure, didn't you?" Mama asked, as she backed the car around and drove onto the street.

"Yes! How on earth did you know?"

She chuckled. "Mothers know everything. Well, almost everything; you nearly jumped out of your skin when the curator took it out to show us. Now, tell me about it."

So I told her. I was still telling her when we got home to our big Victorian house, and I kept on telling while Mama made breakfast, and served it to me and my two younger brothers and Daddy as well.

"What's all this about?" he asked. "What did the curator have to show you?"

"A *Christkindl* figure; a really important find," she said, and began to tell him the story over again. When she finished, Daddy looked at her, and then at me, and then he pushed back from the table and said to my brothers, "Come on, guys, let's take advantage of the new snow," and they went outside to make snow people.

"He didn't say a word about what you told him," I said to Mama after they left.

"He's still thinking it over."

"Does he believe me?"

"Of course, what did you think?"

"I just wondered." Then, as I thought about it, I asked her, "Did you believe me?"

"Oh, yes," she answered. "I believed you. But I haven't decided exactly what happened."

"You think it was a dream, don't you?"

"I'm not sure. There may be such a thing as visiting the past. I have a friend who studies that subject. Some remarkable people have written about such experiences, whatever they mean, and however they come about."

"So it might not be a dream?"

"Well," said Mama, "There are dreams, and then again, well—there are dreams!"

"Can a dream be true?"

She reached out then, and laid her hand on mine.

"A German writer once said something about that," she told me.

"What?"

"Let me think. He wrote in the very late eighteenth century; he published under the pen name of Novalis. He said this: 'Our life is no dream; but it ought to become one, and perhaps it will.' I've always thought that was a beautiful idea."

"Was he right?"

"I don't know," Mama answered. "I was hoping you'd be able to tell me."